I0589073

# Bare Feet

## By Sharon Gartner

IBSN 978-0-9873750-9-4

Cover Design- Libbi Reed
www.libbireed.com
Editing Janine Ogden

*An Invisible red thread connects those who are destined to meet, regardless of time, place, or circumstance. The thread may stretch or tangle, but will never break.*

*~ Ancient Chinese belief~*

# 1

*Earth time: 10am.*

*Agenda: Employee assessment meeting of spiritual guides.*
*Place: Guides Incorporated.*
*Location: The other side of physical reality.*
*Present: Rebecca, Elizabeth, Gypsy, Centurion Lizard.*

## Elizabeth

I hate these assessment meetings.

Okay, hate is a fierce word, but there is no other word to describe it. Getting called up to an assessment meeting in our business means you have hit an all-time low in your career. It's a business that doesn't have many rules, regulations, or guidelines; just free of heart guidance for the client on the path they've selected; so to mess that up, well there is only one way to describe it: we *suck* at being spiritual guides.

"Well, well," Rebecca said as she planted herself beside me in the empty chair, "why am I not surprised to see you here?" she smirked, opening her day planner.

Well that's does it, if I hadn't hit rock bottom before, I officially have now.

My arch rival in the business of spiritual guidance is sitting beside me, about to witness the low point of my whole afterlife existence.

Rebecca used to be a PR for one of the top CEOs in New York. When she passed over her laptop and day planner seemed to arrive with her. My money is on the fact she probably requested to get buried with them so as not to miss a deadline or memo. And ever since she arrived here, she self-appoints herself for everything, including taking notes for this meeting. If I could punch her in the face I would.

"Well if you gave us decent clients to begin with Rebecca," I sneered back, "we wouldn't have to face the wrath of the spiritual council."
"Well if you reined in your need for control Elizabeth you wouldn't be here," she smirked.
Oh my god, that is the pot calling the kettle black. But I'm not about to tell her it's got nothing to do with control, it was about initiative.

I mean it was out of my control that John the spinster accountant decided to jump out of a plane on the day the apprentice parachute packer had a hangover; which led to parachute failure, causing his physical body into an early death. I only pushed him into skydiving 'cos he was so totally boring; I thought it was the incentive he needed to get him out of his comfort zone.

I just thought a little excitement wouldn't go astray. And I must add it wouldn't have happened if Rebecca had assigned me a client that wasn't so boring. I mean all I did is sit around all day and watch as he punched numbers into a computer. I was never going to get any further ahead in this business with a client like that. God, I swear Rebecca does that on purpose to make herself look better.

"Would you stop saying 'God'," Rebecca hissed at me, "I can hear your thoughts from here. You'll get yourself in more trouble using her name in blaspheme."
"Oh my god Rebecca, you're such an arse kisser."

Rebecca quickly scribbles something down on paper and slaps it in front of me.
"Your aggressive attitude is now officially on report," she said, placing her pen back in her top pocket, "this is your first official warning."

Oh seriously, she would have just made that up, this is what I'm talking about, self-important, master-of-nothing. Well she can kiss my arse.

"Actually Elizabeth," she turned to me in all her hoity-ness, "as from this morning I have the authority to issue warnings and report anyone I see as incompetent to the High Council. That, in front of you, is the official warning on an official letterhead. So *you* can kiss *my* arse."

I really must learn to block mind readers, especially her warped and twisted mind.

Rebecca shoots me a glare.

Boss cleared his throat from the head of the round table. Boss, who also answers to 'Bossman', is a tribesman from ancient times and he's only just been promoted.

But at least he wears a poncho these days, I remember when I first passed over and he met me at the gates wearing nothing but what I would describe as a swimsuit made from fur and bone. And Bossman is no oil painting in the looks department, so the sight of his naked self in a tribesman bathing suit was to much that the Spiritual Guides Union moved that the office dress policy, regardless of what era you came from, requires you to wear clothing from neck to knees. (And closed-in footwear around headquarters.)

"Okay everyone," Bossman's deep booming voice carried through the room, "if you would all be seated let's gets started... where is Jesus?"

"He's refusing to come out of his room again," said Gypsy like she didn't care she was about to face his wrath for being lazy. "He's swamped under with requests and on his 'wish they would leave me alone' rant."

"Price of fame," the Centurion Lizard tutted sadly, whacking his heavy tail on the ground.

"Well then I'll have a word to the High Council, it may mean Jesus will have to be retired to the In-Between," Bossman said.

God there is no room for error in this place, miss attending a meeting and it's instant forced retirement.

"Lisa! The G word!" Rebecca hissed under her breath.

"We have a situation," Bossman continued, waving his hand so the big projector screen appears in front of us, "please observe."

And there we were, all of us present, except Rebecca, flashing like a disco ball on the big screen.

Gypsy; seen fast asleep in the passenger seat of her client's car, failing to warn him about the oncoming out-of-control hay truck.

Centurion Lizard; who has spent years in hiding because his cowardly arse couldn't negotiate peace with the different races and resulted in years of wars.

And then there was me; sitting on John the accountant's desk, bored shitless and filing my nails. Okay I shouldn't have put that skydiving brochure in front of him or influenced his equally boring office staff to buy him the gift voucher, but the guy needed a little adrenalin rush, all he ever did is push a pen and eat TV dinners in front of Antiques Road Show, even his sexual desire was as routine as his annual tax return as it's not like he had a wife.

But I have to admit I may have pushed it a little too far. All I wanted was a promotion; a chance to do something else rather than guide people in their mundane lives, I wanted to be the guide that other spiritual guides look up to.
And yes, okay, if I had been paying attention to the young hung-over parachute packer instead of checking out the hot skydiving instructor, I could have avoided John's death, but it's not like he isn't having a good time, I mean he's gotten to see his mother again.

But unfortunately John's death will set off a chain reaction of events that have to be altered. For example John now will never cross paths with Rose, who would never get to receive the invite to John's cousin's wedding after finding the invitation and a note in her tax return (compliments of yours truly).

Which would have resulted in her accepting the bewildered John's invitation, where she would have been introduced to Beth, who shared her passion for theatre and who would've encouraged her to go for the part of Cathy in the musical of Wuthering Heights, which she would have gotten. That would have then started the career that she always dreamed of.

And of course John would have gotten laid.

This job is so underrated!

The screen disappears and we all shift uncomfortably in our seats as Bossman retrieves his trademark stick from its resting place at the edge of the round table.

If you ever have that feeling when your mind goes blank or you forget why you walked into a room, chances are it would be Bossman whacking you round the head with his stick, it's not brutal, it's because you're about to make a wrong turn or need to change the course of events.

But I'm now feeling a tad nervous. Okay, so what we did was not that bad, but bad enough that we are sitting here; there is only one option for those who mess up, and that is the In-Between. It's not a horrible place, it's just like clipping the wings on a chicken, you can't fly anywhere and you're not assigned to do anything; just sit around and observe for, well, eternity.

I'm too young and intelligent to go there, and besides it's full of old smelly spirits, a bit like earth's retirement homes.

Bossman lets out a sigh; I can sense Lizard is trying hard to contain his tears.

Bossman leans heavily on his stick.

"Your incompetency has left very bad consequences for many, not to mention the loss of faith in us from those still in the physical world; and many paths have been destroyed. It saddens me," Bossman lowered his head.

And when he does that, the guilt that fills us is overwhelming, it's to make us realise the pain we have caused by our actions.

Oh god, that's it, Lizard has lost it.

"I-I-I'm sssorry," Lizard sobbed, "but it's not m,m,my fault, people are just not listening these d,d,days."

"Oh please," Gypsy scoffed at him, "you've had like millions of years to sort your shit out, what about what I've had to put up with? I've been with the same guy for 67 years trying to teach him the same lesson day in and day out, banging my head against a wall trying to get through to him, and he still hasn't learned what he needs to learn."

"Well he can't now he's dead," Rebecca smirked, vigorously taking notes.

"Oh really Gypsy," Lizard said in his dry tone despite his tears, "well bring out the violins, if you hadn't been asleep for 60 of those 67 years, you may have actually achieved something."

Ohhhh I can feel a fight coming on.

"Well, need I remind you," Gypsy retorted, "it was you who crashed that spaceship, causing a big bang and wiping out your own kind."

"Silence!!!" Bossman yelled, slamming his stick on the table in front of us and causing us to jump. "We are all at fault for negatively altering the course of a few lives. It's a mad world out there, both in physical and spirit form. Paths get crossed all the time and clients temporarily stray from their paths, yes it happens, and most of the time it is corrected as you are well aware. But you lot have either been weak in your duties or have interfered with the course of action set out by your clients."

I hang my head in shame as Bossman looks in my direction at that last statement.

"But despite your weakness," he continued, "the High Council has selected you all for an important task."

Stunned silence falls over the table; obviously none of us had seen this one coming. I can even feel Rebecca's dumbfounded pause of her pen upon hearing the news. We have been selected by the High Council, that involves God herself; this has to be important.

And she chose *us*.

"This mission comes with rewards; succeed and you will be put forward for promotion. This is Cameron," Bossman goes on without a pause, pulling the projector screen back down out of thin air as Lizard, Gypsy and myself shoot glances of shock at each other. The image reveals a heavy-set man who appeared to be driving a rig.

"He is 44, single, and has had a lot of bad luck with past relationships," Bossman continued, "he has endured all his hard lessons he needed to learn in this life to walk his path well, but unfortunately it has left him with a fear of woman and he does not believe in love, so we need to help him renew a belief in love and life."

Okay now I'm confused, that seems pretty mundane and not so important, everyone has some bad luck in their relationships, it's often a past life thing.

Oh my god, please don't tell me this is another lame client who cannot see his own faults through a haze of repeated mistakes.

Rebecca thumps another piece of paper in front of me.
*'Final warning for using the G word in blasphemy'.*
Oh for god's sake.

The screen flashes to a new imagine of a fair headed woman who is arranging what looks like a bunch of lilies.

"... and this is Kym, his soul mate and future wife," Bossman continues, "in this life she is 40 years old and has given up finding her Mr Right. Note her biological clock has nearly expired so you have to move fast as their genes have been programmed to produce little Phoenix."
Another image flashes on the screen of a new born baby boy.

"Phoenix is vital to this earth, as his brain and talents will revolutionise the way the planet exists; it is extremely important he is conceived."
"And what sort of things will this Phoenix be achieving?" asked Rebecca as she continues to write in her book in front of her.

"I have been advised that information is classified and there is no reason to know how important this young soul is to us, your part is to unite these two beings. You will not fail at this mission!" he paused so the message can sink in.

I turn my head and pretend to look at the screen to hide my expression of alarm. If the order has come from God herself and little Phoenix is the saviour of mankind, then this is huge; and why us?

Gypsy and Lizard have been guides longer than I have so yes they have experience but they are not very good at it.

But this is an opportunity for me to prove my worth and work up the corporate ladder, then I will be doing the big stuff like diverting wars and consulting with Mother Nature as to which natural disaster will happen. None of this helping people who cannot make up their minds stuff, who contently ask the universe for material things thinking it's going to make them happy. Hell this could even be an opportunity to outshine Rebecca, then she would really have to kiss my butt.

He throws a folder on the middle of the table.

"Here is the file on them both, please study it and come up with the best way to make this happen.

Rebecca will personally oversee this mission and report back to me on a daily basis."

"What?" Rebecca gasps as she all of a sudden stops her flurry of writing.

"Yes Rebecca, this mission will be fully supervised by you; you will be my eyes and ears on the ground. Of course I shall be watching from up here but I need a leader on the ground."

Ha! So this is news to Rebecca, even her perfect sensory intuition didn't pick up on this one, this will knock her ego for a six.

"But with this lot?" Rebecca stuttered, "with all due respect Bossman, they are not exactly capable of handling anything."

"High Council believes this team is perfect to see this through," Bossman said in a no-nonsense tone, "you have two weeks earth time to complete it, we don't normally work on earth time but this is critical. Rebecca follow me for a briefing please."

Rebecca slowly rises from her seat and follows Bossman, leaving us to process the news.

Wow.

I mean wow!

"I don't want to go to the In-Between," Lizard sobs again in a panic, pulling me from my state of shock.

"What makes you think we are going to be sent to the In-Between?" asks Gypsy irritably, "wouldn't mind it myself, all they do is sleep and people watch."

"I just can't. Oh man how we are going to pull this off? And if we do pull this off, I don't want a promotion, that's more responsibility. Oh lord I can't breathe."

"Okay," I said out loud, gathering my thoughts as Lizard breathes into a paper bag, "let's just start at the beginning."


I picked up Cameron's file and flicked through the pages. Not bad-looking but not real hot either, nice eyes I suppose. Let's see, 44, every girlfriend he's ever had has tended to betray him in some way... blah, blah, blah, same old story, same old lesson, my god why can't they come up with something new.

Drives trucks and is scared of birds.

Pfft no wonder he's got a fear of women, he sits in an isolated cab 90% of the time.

Okay just caught a glimpse of his history, he was caged up as a slave by a queen in a past life so that explains that one.

Easily fixed.

Doesn't explain the fear of birds, think that may come from being attacked by roosters in his childhood.

What else?

Hasn't had sex in 9 months.

Boring.

Closing his folder and chucking it back on the table I picked up the next one. Lizard and Gypsy start to bicker across the table about something that happened last century.

Those two really must stop living in the past.

Rebecca hasn't come back yet which gives me a chance to get a head start and come up with my own plan.

Okay let's see if Kym is more interesting.

She looks all of her 40 years, wears glasses; should be wearing contacts, glasses do not suit her at all. Fair hair, hmmm few highlights wouldn't go astray; manages a florist shop, takes hay-fever tablets - ironic. Given up on finding Mr Right due to lack of interest in relationships.

Pfff I think this assignment is not as tough as what Mr Bossman is making it out to be and he is just trying to scare us into succeeding in this mission by all the talk of little Phoenix's important role to humanity.

I mean my god how hard is it to get two people together? I do it all the time, too easy.

I don't see why everyone is in such a state of panic.

Rebecca reappears holding a takeaway foam coffee cup which causes Lizard to flash his 'rage colours'.

"Oh get over it," Rebecca scorned at him, "it's an environmentally friendly cup."

She clears her throat in order to bide her time because all of a sudden Rebecca has to step beyond the office and up the task of assigning guides to humans, real work.

"Okay we will split into two teams, Gypsy and Lizard you take Cameron."

"What!?" protested Gypsy while Lizard proceeds to blow into the bag again.

Rebecca continues, ignoring the outcries.

"Get a plan going on how you are going to guide him towards Kym; he drives a truck so find out if he makes deliveries in her area, if he doesn't then you need to redirect things."

Gypsy's in a huff and Lizard's really flashing his rage colours now.

Wish he wouldn't do that, it's like a bloody 70s disco in here.

But if those two have been assigned to Cameron then there's only one option left for me.

"Elizabeth will guide Kym," Rebecca continued, "and of course I shall be overseeing all of you."

Bloody hell, why do I get the female, men are so much easier, men just accept what they have been told or in this case, altered, to do; women have to analyse things until their hair falls out and of course the only reason Rebecca wants me to be with this Kym is 'cos she knows damn well how much harder it will be. Seriously it does not take two guides to guide a man.

"Actually Elizabeth," Rebecca snapped turning to me as if she is about to explode with the pressure, "the Centurion here is big, scaly, and can redirect a 30 tonne truck physically, Gypsy has had experience with all things travelling so it makes sense they take on the male client as he is a flippin' truck driver."

I really must get on to blocking her from reading my thoughts, I mean how the bloody hell does she do it, we're not supposed to be able to in our position, plus we wouldn't be able to hear ourselves think through the noise of others.

But knowing Rebecca she probably created her own mind reading app on the stupid Blackberry thing she carries with her.

"And another reason Elizabeth," she continues as she shoves copies of the mission documents into a folder, "you have a weakness for young men, that's how you stuffed up last time, and the time before that, so I will NOT have you assigned to a male client on my watch! Tomorrow morning, on earth, don't be late," she snapped before stomping out of the room.

I go to open my mouth in protest at her absurd remarks but it's too late. Now I am mad. I mean it's not like this Cameron is young, 44 is not young, well, not the young I'm talking about.
And I don't have a 'weakness' as she puts it, I just have good taste in the young male human figure. Well can you blame me? I died in my prime.
Well this time I won't fail, in fact I will go above and beyond what this mission entails and leave Rebecca in the dust as far as promotion goes.

2

**Cameron**

So here I am, driving down the bumpiest fucking highway in the state, towing a trailer which has had a flat tyre for the last 150 kilometres, wearing half my fucking breakfast down the front of myself after trying to eat the bastard while being thrown around in this cab; and all because they can't build a decent road out of their arse; then I get a call from the depot telling me I have to pick up a load of fucking flowers.

What the fuck? I cart frozen meat.

Apparently some poor prick decided to wrap his flower truck around a pole; he wasn't hurt, and they can't work out how he managed to do it on a straight bit of road, the straightest bit of highway in this whole fucking state actually. Got me stuffed as well; think he must have been sucking on his poppies.

And according to the gossip on the two-way I don't think *he* even knows what the fuck happened.

Sounds like drugs to me. I mean he said something about an 8 metre tall thing with a snout and a tail running out at him.

Yep, definitely drugs.

Anyway, so being the only person use to driving refrigerated trucks in the area and the company I drive for being the only fleet of trucks on this planet (yeah I know, I'm being a sarcastic prick), I landed the fucking job. But why they want a meat truck driver to cart a load of flowers halfway up the state so some bloody festival of bloody flowers can have a bit of colour is beyond me. I mean can't they produce their own bloody flowers? That's just poor bloody planning as far as I'm concerned.

Don't need this aggravation!

Haven't got the full details of the job yet but I guess the first thing I need to do is unload this bloody meat, find out where to from there, and get some sleep if I'm driving for two fucking days straight.

I'm about to come up onto a particular piece of highway which I think of as the dreaded memory lane. Don't know what it is, but every time I drive down this particular road I start thinking about my bloody ex-girlfriend, and how I wasted five years of my bloody life with someone who didn't want kids. Cannot understand why the fuck she couldn't have told me that after the first date and not wait until five fucking years later when I was pushing 43.

That's the part that shits me, I don't care if she was more interested in her gym instructor than me (well obviously, considering she ran off and shacked up with the tosser), but real lousy to lead someone on to believe they are ready to start a family and then run off to the doctor behind ones back to make sure it doesn't happen. Then after 4 years of trying and wondering if my bits and pieces were actually firing properly she finally admitted the whole baby scene is not exactly what she wants in life; it's just beyond a sick joke.

So yeah given the circumstances, not to mention all the other relationship fuck-ups I've had, I'm not exactly Mr Happy these days. Yep as far as woman go, I'm over the lot of them, and if I could turn gay right now I fucking would.
Even though blokes are not much better.

Bad memory lane now behind me, I fight the gearbox yet again to find at least one gear without crunching all 18 of them ('cos that's the kind of shit that happens on this piece of highway) I start thinking about this next job. Haven't carted flowers before, so don't know why the boss wants me to bloody start now. Could have been because the last guy that loaded my truck called me a miserable bastard and threatened to phone my boss and ask if he could send a happier driver, maybe the little bastard wasn't joking.

But if the boss wants these flowers carted up north then that's a two day round trip; well, could do it in 24 hours but the law requires me to drive 12 hours at a time so factor in 7 hours sleep and you may as well say 2 days.

I haven't done those sorts of hours since getting Eliah and Jay-Jay, not sure how they would cope being left on their own for a couple of days.

Eliah and Jay-Jay are my two cats and the only living things that haven't managed to screw me over in any way. Eliah was the first one I got but I felt kind-of sorry for him being inside all day (don't like them going outside, I mean what if something happened to them), so I built him an outside enclosure, it's just an extension off the side of the house so I can open the back door and they have access. Then I felt bad leaving him all on his own so I ended up getting Jay-Jay for company.

My neighbours are under the impression that I built the cat enclosure to protect the wildlife so they think I'm a bit of a tree hugger. That's about as crazy as the guy in the packing room at the meat works who's a vegetarian.

I couldn't give a rats arse about the birds, hate the feathered things, can't stand their flapping; in fact it gives me the shits whenever I'm near the beach and they gather in flocks to scavenge fucking food off any dumb person willing to feed them. Yeah try to avoid the beach if I can, well, don't really go there at all. So apparently I have some sort of phobia to birds that, according to my mother's psychiatrist, stemmed from constant attack from the family rooster as a child.

Maybe I just don't like fucking birds.

So anyway not looking forward to this trip and hoping that the boss doesn't make a habit of volunteering me for any more special sideline jobs.

*Operation KymCam commences.*

**Elizabeth**

Really ready to kill Rebecca. If it were possible.

Rebecca has never revealed to anyone how she died, but right now if I found out she had been murdered on earth I wouldn't be giving her killer the winning lottery numbers for sending her to me.

Bring on day 14 when this is over and I don't have to be in her company. She is smothering me beyond my comfort levels, and not hearing any ideas I have to offer, so from now on, it's game on.

We are in the flower shop and this 'Kym' is a not going to be as easy as I thought. She is what we call a 'qualmy'; someone who questions and doubts all their decisions. Pain in the arse really as it's twice as much work for us 'every decision and feeling comes from their own intuition centre. And instead acting on that 'feeling' the first time and actually doing it, they have to stop and question it, which means a series of repeated probing and redirecting until they actually do a complete circle and realise their first feeling was right.

It's only been a few hours and this girl is already hard work, I'm exhausted.

"Why is it every time I turn around you're just sitting there?" Rebecca hissed, appearing in front of me as I prop myself up on the front counter of the shop to observe the physical people around me, it can be kinda fun knowing what lies ahead of them, and the fact they have no clue.

"There's nothing more to do for now," I said, rolling my eyes at her, "and besides at least I'm actually awake, take a look at her normal guide over there in the corner, I mean how old is she, 105?"

"That's her great granny," Rebecca hissed, "she's been watching over her for the last 40 years, I told her to take some time off! Now has Kym received the last minute order for the festival of flowers?"

"Yes."

"Has she rung the right transport company?"

"Yes, Gypsy manipulated all the transport companies within a 100km radius so they won't be available and Lizard is now resting his scaly knee after injuring it pushing the flower truck off the road," I sighed, disinterested.

"And you're sure it's Cameron's truck scheduled to pick up this delivery tomorrow morning?" continued Rebecca, scrolling down a list she has on a clipboard, ticking off every task as it's completed.

She has all this power as a spiritual being and yet she still acts like she is in the physical world with all her pathetic stationary needs. If I really cared, I would have suggested she was a materialistic person in the physical world but I don't care so I never ask her about that side of her past life.

"Yes it's all good. Again. Time out Rebecca."

She glares at me before moving off.

I go back to my task of watching this 'Kym' and I have to say she doesn't do herself any justice with her hair, in fact it's like she's given up on her appearance altogether. How is Cameron going to even give her a second look when she looks so drab. He's a male, first impressions count, so think a trip to the hairdresser for some highlights is on the agenda.

Actually come to think of it, bet ya she hasn't maintained anything else either.

Hmmm maybe I should take a peak.

Nah, that's a bit invasive, even for us. Maybe I should just check the legs instead.

"Elizabeth what are you doing?" Rebecca re-appeared, along with her pit-bull attitude.

"I was just checking if she shaves her legs. I mean you're the one that said do whatever it takes. Well in my opinion having hairy legs is not going to attract any man."

"It's going to happen anyway, it's a path that has been written for them regardless of vanity Elizabeth, that's just you interfering again."

"I beg to differ," I mumbled, "it's called 'thinking outside the square'."

"Need I remind you, *that* is the reason you are in this position?" Rebecca snapped, "your last incentive resulted in no more client. Now all we have to do is make sure they meet, so is Kym going to be here in the morning when Cameron arrives for the delivery?"

God maybe she was the fun police in her earth life.

"Elizabeth?"

"Yes, god, yes she will be here."

"Will you stop with the G word!" Rebecca snapped. "Now that's all that needs to happen, so make sure it does. If you'll excuse me I must report back to Bossman. I trust you will do as you are asked and stay with this woman?"

She is really doing my head in. I don't care what she says, I think I need to probe this Kym into a makeover, I mean this assignment is pretty much sorted anyway.

 Tomorrow Cameron will come and pick up the flowers and Kym will make sure he has signed off on the delivery invoice, and their eyes will meet and they will hook up and make lots of love and a baby.

Too easy.

I mean Rebecca hasn't even booked cupid's services so it must be pretty straight-forward.

And this is my issue; this assignment may very well be over and done with tomorrow, Rebecca will report back to Bossman that the mission is complete, she will be recognised for her good work, Cameron and Kym will be united, Gypsy can go back to sleep and Lizard can go back to burying his head in the sand, what will become of me? Probably be promoted to ticking off names at the pearly gates. No, this assignment may not be a hard one but I can improve it.

Kym obviously hasn't had any proper guidance, that part is evident by her sleeping great granny in the corner; her hair, her clothes, in fact her whole plain-Jane demeanour suggests to me she hasn't stepped outside her comfort zone since she came out of her mother's womb.

And what of her destiny? Meeting a guy and raising a child? Okay so yes I understand this may be her path but this is the difference between being promoted or not.

Because not only would I have saved humanity, I would have saved one plain-Jane from living a life not reaching her full potential. It's just a slight tweaking. And I would be doing her a huge favour; how good would it feel to start a new relationship looking and feeling good.

That settles it; I have decided to do it. First thing in the morning, full Brazilian and leg wax, as well as a hair trim complemented by bronze highlights. Be done by midday and back in the shop in time for Cameron to arrive to pick up the flowers.

Too easy.

**Kym**

A bit chilly out this evening but I do enjoy my evening walk home, gives me a chance to unwind from the day. And, oh my, what a day. It started out fairly normal until I had the strangest phone call from the Mooranba Regional Council which is upstate from here, quite a considerable way up actually, but turns out the 3000 orchids they had ordered as the theme for their town display to highlight their annual spring festival, ended up flattened on the side of the highway. Which is a bit of a pity as orchids can be extremely hard to get sometimes, especially as they are coming to the end of their season, so they have asked if my little florist's shop would fill the order.

Apparently I came highly recommend to them by some unknown source that no job is too big. I have to say I was flattered they chose my shop if not a bit puzzled as 'no job too big' has never been my motto; and I actually cannot understand why they didn't go to a wholesaler or a market, I mean there must be a dozen more capable florist shops between here and there. It seemed an awfully impossible task; 3000 orchids at such short notice and I was about to gracefully turn the order down until I spied the note that my work experience girl had written down. A phone number of her uncle, who was not only the president of the orchid society but grew them himself as well.

So one quick phone call to him and in two hours we managed to round up 3000 beautiful flowers to be sent to the Spring Flower Festival in Mooranba. Seemed very coincidental, but oh well, these things happen.

Yes, so I have never actually transported flowers that far before so I guess to keep them fresh I'd need to use a refrigerated transporter, but they seem to be as rare as hens teeth, which is also strange as the highways are riddled with refrigerated trucks. Also did not help that some of the yellow pages were torn out of my business directory, let me assure you I shall be getting to the bottom of that when I find the perpetrator, but I did manage to find one transport company who seemed a bit whishy washy about transporting flowers but agreed to deliver.

So tomorrow will be an extremely busy day as the order will be delivered to the shop first thing in the morning after they are picked fresh so it can be packed carefully and on its way by the afternoon. I'm so pleased I have Tamara, my work experience student, here to help me, I'm also hoping my friend Mandy will help as well. Luckily I have some space in the back room to use as a temporary packing shed; I'm still starting to wonder what I have gotten myself in for though.

As I turned the corner into my street I started to analyse my life; I'm really not what you'd call a joyful person, I certainly don't lead a very exciting life. If I was honest with myself I could say I never really wanted to own a florist shop, although I love flowers, they were never my passion.

It started off a pet store then evolved into a florist shop that still kept and sold birds and aquarium fish. I was never really one for fish but birds I love, have done so since I was a child, something about how graceful they are, they're truly a magnificent creation. So for a while after I took over, I kept a section of the shop for exotic birds.

I brought the shop because it was close to where I was living and it was enough to support me. I have no children and was not very successful in the romantic department; most men seem to think a single woman without children is only after one thing and that is children, so they tend to run. I also found it very hard with communication and never found anyone I could relate to on an intellectual level, so I have simply given up on the whole dating thing, seems less complicated. Not that I am some hot-shot university graduate, in fact, I only just muddled through high school.

I spent many of my years at high school with my head down, not really wanting to get to know anyone. Yes you could say I'm a bit of a loner, don't get me wrong I had friends but I really didn't share their enthusiasm for things like boys, clothes or makeup.

I didn't see the point, waste of energy really. That was here today, gone tomorrow sort of stuff. I was into books and sitting watching bird documentaries; so when I left high school I volunteered my time at the state library until eventually they gave me a job and I went on to become Head Librarian.

I stayed until I brought the shop five years ago with the help of my friend Mandy (whose cottage I rent at the back of her property) as it was her quest to get me out of my shell and in to a job that actually talks to people. So I took her advice and brought the shop and now here I am.

So that's me in a nutshell.

The smell of Mandy's home cooking hits me as I pass her kitchen window making my way to the little flat behind her house. The flurry of children's voices and dinner plates clanging is an all-too-familiar sound on my daily journey home, but the routine of it all is very comforting to me. Mandy is a single parent with three children, a hero in my eyes; the oldest has behavioural problems and her twin girls can also be a challenge at times. They were only babies when I first met her when she endured a breakdown in the middle of the children's section of the library after discovering her husband had left her for another woman and her 4 year old had tipped the twins baby formula down his underwear.

I took her back to my office and gave her a cup of coffee, mainly to get her out of the main part of the library, but I seemed to have an instant nurturing bond with this lady and her children, and we have been close ever since. I moved into the flat out the back of her place to help her out with the bills and for us to keep each other company, so yes, it's a friendship I value very much.

As I unlock the door to my humble pad I am reminded again of how uneventful my life is and a pang of loneliness hits me. But unless cupid hits me with the love bug, highly unlikely, then it's just me and my beloved birds.

Strange, having the overwhelming urge to clean out my wardrobe.

**Elizabeth**

Okay things are way worse than I thought. This woman has the most boring clothes in the world.

She really must do something about that now!

No wonder men get put off her, I mean for starters the woman lives with a bunch of birds, has a collection of encyclopaedias, and a draw full of stockings.

And not the sexy type either.

It was so boring I was tempted to go and see what the lady with the kids was up to as there seemed to be a lot more fun happening over there. But no, I spent the whole night waiting for Kym to go to sleep. She didn't even turn the TV on; she just sat with her ticking clock and her birds and read a book.

But now it's dawn and after an entire night whispering in her ear and altering her thought patterns, I'm hoping I have done enough to convince her she needs to book in a hair appointment before meeting Cameron.

And not a moment too soon I say, I mean everyone experiences major changes at least once in their life and she is so overdue for hers.

Wonder why the High Council chose this time in Kym's life to alter her journey. I mean if this happened 5 years ago there wouldn't be the urgency to get her laid and pregnant before her ovaries dry up.

God only knows why the archangels and spiritual guides don't work with earth time.

We do have some insight into our client's future, that's why people go to those psychics and have readings. Physical humans do have the ability to communicate with their guides but most just don't know how (or even believe we exist, pfft) so they have to seek expert help. It can be frustrating; if they only knew to listen to themselves they could save a whole lot of money anyway.

So yes we do have some insights like I have with Kym here, but it's a path that is set before she was born and our job is to guide her along. The path is not always guaranteed and people can change their direction. With over 7 billion people on the planet and over 180 billion spirit guides from all the people that've gone before, floating around, things are bound to get muddled. But I know all will work out with Kym and if no one interferes (and it's my job to make sure they don't) then things will go smoothly.

Rebecca has been back a few times through the night to check on me just to make sure I'm still here. She thinks I cannot see her as she sneaks round, but she forgets she's not the only one that is practiced at that. It's going to be tough tomorrow trying to keep Rebecca out of my way while I get this lady to a hairdresser, but I have a plan so just have to have faith in my abilities.

Gypsy and Lizard apparently are also instructed to stay with the truck driver until the 'meeting of the two souls' happens, as Rebecca is putting it; not a good name for a business project and she should stop before she really embarrasses herself.

The movement next to me indicates Kym is awakening from her night's sleep. Oh my god this is so exciting, I just hope she listens to her intuition centre 'cos boy I planted a lot of seeds in there. Cannot wait to see her with her new look. Also cannot wait to prove Rebecca wrong.

I sat patiently while she went through her normal routine of herbal tea and muesli while listening to some boring talkback radio station; it's like an old musty 1950s home in here, absolutely no energy whatsoever.
Think I need to change that as well. Bit of paint wouldn't go astray. Funky the place up a bit.

I focus on something on the wall trying to pass the time and wait for her to go to the bathroom so she can look in the mirror and decide she should book at the hairdressers.

I wish she would hurry up as I have already arranged a last minute appointment slot for her by arranging a cancellation (which by the way takes a lot of planning and work as you have to alter another person's daily path to suit), but this is a top class hairdressing salon and I'm sure the appointment time I managed to snag for her will fill up fast if she's too slow getting on to it, especially when there are other guides out there working hard for their people. I cannot control everything that happens behind the scenes, it's a dog-eat-dog place here in the spirit world.

I'm staring at a spot on the wall when Lizard appears, every time he shows up it's like a sonic boom through your soul, his presence is so bold.

"What are you doing here?" I hiss, trying to feel my heartbeat then remembering it's long gone. "If Rebecca sees you here, she'll go bananas."

"She knows I'm here, she sent me to check if everything's going smoothly and to see if you have the subject out of bed yet."

I cannot speak of how offended I am right now, how dare she send the scaly one to check up on me.

"Well you can tell 'Miss Snotty Rebecca' that everything's under control 'cos I actually do some work and don't just climb up the High Council's arse."

"Not sure I'm allowed to swear at her," said Lizard in a panic. "Please don't make me tell her that."

Oh for goodness sake.

"Fine, I'll write her a note."

While I'm sorting out Lizard's message he takes a quick look around. Kym's birds can sense his presence and are chirping at the top of their feathered lungs, he really needs to leave; he is causing such a disturbance.

Lizard's looking a bit alarmed.

Kym starts to move from her seat, I really must follow her actions in the next 5 minutes so I quickly scribble something down and hand it back to Lizard.

"Um Elizabeth I'm a bit concerned about something."

"Not now!" I hissed, "I have to follow her."

"Yes but this shouldn't wait," said Lizard, "it's just that I don't think..."

God Kym has gone into the bathroom.

"Tell me later," I hissed, "now shoo, take the note back to Rebecca, I'm busy, just tell her everything's good at this end and we may be slightly late but it's all good."

I disappear through the bathroom door and catch Kym looking in the mirror in horror as she fluffs her hair; I quietly sidle up next to her and whisper the name of the hairdresser.
I'm waiting with bated breath to see if it works as guiding someone is one thing, altering thought patterns and behaviour is another.
Her hand flops to her side and she sighs a huge sigh.

I had slipped a hairdressing card on the bathroom counter the night before for more inspiration. Her eyes suddenly catch the card and she picks it up and stares at it for the longest time before disappearing from the bathroom. I turn to follow her when Rebecca appears in front of me waving Lizard's message in the air.
"So we're all fine over here then?" she says in a stern matron's voice, trying to be intimidating and acting like I'm in trouble for writing her a note stating that crawling up the High Council's backside must be exhausting.
"Yes all good here," I said, smiling my sweetest smile back.

"Don't stuff it up Elizabeth, all my senses are tingling a warning that you're up to something."

Damn I tried to block that, must work on my shield.

"So promise me you will have Kym there and unblock any obstacle in her path."

Rebecca almost looks like she is pleading with me, this must really mean a lot to her; well, this promotion means a lot to me too, so my plan stays.

"I promise," I said, trying not to sound irritated, last thing I need right now is to get Rebecca's back up. That would only force her not to leave my side.

She leaves with a look of distrust in her eyes and I strengthen my shield so she cannot tune into what I'm about to do.

She disappears from my vision just as I see Kym throwing clothes from her wardrobe like she has lost something.

# 3

## Kym

I had the strangest dream last night that I was heavily pregnant and I was on a train with people all around me and they all looked miserable, then all of a sudden I was pushing out a baby and I gave birth right there on the train and all the faces turned to ashes.

But the strangest thing of all is when I woke up I felt really odd, it's like I cannot stand being in my own skin.

So here I am on the busiest day my little shop has had since it was nothing but foundations on the ground, sitting in a hairdressing salon while I'm being talked into cutting my long straight mousy brown hair into a feathered bob with bronze highlights.

It's so absurd it's almost funny.

Even my birds were acting weird this morning; I had to leave them partially covered just to keep them calm. Sammy, my pet galah, had even started to pull his own feathers out.

But despite the chaos, surprisingly it feels, well kinda good in a scary way. I wasn't planning to come out to the hairdressers when I should be at the shop helping poor Tamara but I just couldn't stand my hair any longer.

If anything, it would be good to help control the mop that re-occurs every time we get a little humidity in the air, which in summer is just about every day, and it'll cut down on the cost of conditioner. So I saw the card Mandy must have left on my bathroom vanity and thought 'why not'?

I was lucky as there was a cancellation today so they managed to squeeze me in, apparently you usually have to make an appointment weeks in advance.

How times have changed. I'm a little embarrassed to say this but I haven't been to a hairdresser since my sister's wedding and she has just celebrated her 14th anniversary.

So when the hairdresser asked me what was I after, I was in complete panic as I have never thought about it so I decided to leave, and just when I got up to leave I spied this model in a magazine opened next to my bag. She was sporting a feather bob style and I just fell in love with it.

I feel surreal as I never do things on impulse.

I asked the lady hairdresser if she could do such a style and before you know it I put my trust in this lady behind me with scissors.

So on the busiest day of my working life, I'm sitting in this hairdressing salon.

It's a good thing Mandy is coming down after she drops the kids off at school but really, me in a hairdressing salon, I'm fighting the urge to giggle.

I'm not sure what's happening, even getting dressed this morning had me wanting to ditch the clothes I have always worn, which is strange as they are incredibly comfortable; as comfortable as my Hush Puppies shoes. But as I was on my way to the hairdressers I saw the most beautiful summer dress in the window of a boutique store and had the overwhelming desire to go in and try it on.

But I really must get my thoughts back on track and get back to the shop, I phoned Tamara before (this salon is a bit flash and as I don't own a mobile phone they bought a phone to me while I was getting my hair cut) and she has informed me the orchids have turned up and Mandy has just arrived to help. Tamara was unsure on how to pack them so I hope the instructions I have left her are not too complicated. When I phoned her back, she assured me everything is fine and the delivery truck is still on schedule to pick them up at 1pm.

I'm starting to panic slightly even though it's only 9am as I really should oversee everything before the truck picks the flowers up. I shouldn't be too much longer anyway as my new haircut seems to be taking shape quickly, this is so exciting.

**Elizabeth**

Okay, it's taken a while and a lot of my energy, but with Rebecca being on my case I thought I would try a little trick that I learnt when I first crossed over.

I'm not supposed to know this trick, but one of the ancient tribal witch-doctors took a liking to me when I arrived at the gates and well, he took me under his wing – literally. Anyway it alters the mind and slows down time so at the moment Rebecca is about an hour behind earth time, she will see everything is working well and that they are an hour ahead of time. It's an illusion and I had already informed Rebecca the subject is having breakfast at her local café, so Rebecca will think Kym is having breakfast for 3 hours and is all good with it 'cos she is in lala land and has no idea how long breakfast takes in earth time. Well she once did, but since crossing over, like a lot of us, has lost an accurate sense of time.

Okay yes, it's witchcraft and we are not allowed to practice anything that gives an illusion but this is Phoenix we are talking about, saviour of the earth, so by all means possible. I'm sure Phoenix doesn't want a mother with hairy legs and no ambition, what kind of a role model would that be.

I'm watching the hairdresser like a hawk, if she gets distracted then there goes the whole time schedule thing, time-keeping is exhausting, no wonder physical humans are stressed all day long, slave to a round thing that goes tick tock, controlling their every move. I had to get here ahead of Kym and get hold of the hairdressers spirit guide; a middle aged man that appears to be from the 80s punk era. He stands by her side and watches her cut hair day in and day out. Maybe it's karmic duty for ruining his curly locks when he decided to become a punk; either way he wasn't too impressed I was interfering and I must have a word to Bossman that if he is putting me on a 'classified mission' then I want a special badge that states it so I can flash it around when I try to explain a situation to another spirit guide about why I want him to step away from his client.

Punk guy is annoyed I mucked up his client's day by arranging an early morning booking, so it took a lot of sweet talking on my part to convince him it's for a greater good and to please stand aside while I get this over with. Even so, he is watching me like a hawk. Rebecca hasn't turned up yet so the illusion of time must be still working. Gypsy informs me the truck will be at the shop 1pm earth time, so far so good as it's only 9am.

Once she gets this done I've arranged for a beauty clinic around the corner to have space for a quick leg and eyebrow wax before we pop past a boutique store to buy a dress that was placed in the shop window last night so could see it (compliments of yours truly).

Once she tries on the dress and decides she will wear it, she'll get to the shop around 11am to show off her new style, Romeo will turn up in his truck, shoot her a glance, she will carry on feeling fabulous with her new look and smooth legs, and back to the board room for me where I will get recognised for my little effort, snub my nose at Rebecca, and move to the top of the ladder.

I must say the hair is starting to take shape and I feel truly inspired. Men are different, most are creatures of habit so once they're in a rut it can be hard to pull them out (unless you put them in a plane and make them jump out of it, but let's not re-visit past mistakes) but woman are meant to grow and soar. They are the creators of life and with their multi-tasking skills, can achieve anything; so to see a lady about to transform is like watching a butterfly come out from a cocoon, truly amazing.

Time is going well and I'm contemplating maybe taking a short trip past an interior decorating shop while we are at it to spruce up her apartment,

I mean once Kym gets back to the shop and Cameron arrives to pick up the flowers and their eyes met and blah, blah, then that will be it for me and even if I put in a request to stay with Kym, the application process could take months (earth time) and by then Kym will already probably have given birth to little Phoenix and be in baby mode and I don't really do baby mode.

The sound of the hairdresser's blow dryer fills the air and I check how we are going for time, 9.30am, spot on.
Oh shoot, the hairdresser's spirit guide has appeared at her side and all of a sudden she turns the hairdryer off.
Oh no, now she has excused herself and disappeared out the back of the shop, better deal with this.

"Excuse me," I said with all the business type politeness I can muster. "Your client had not finished with my client, I ask you again Sir, not to interfere."
He turned to me and an 80s punkrocker sneer, that he probably carried when he was alive, came upon his face.
"Tell me again wot your auforityis?"
Oh and he has suddenly turned on a British accent, what a cliché.

"I already told you, I'm on a classified mission sent down here by Bossman himself, and authorised by the High Council.

My client needs to get her hair finished now."

"Yeah well my client needs a new car right, and I've worked really 'ard to get 'er the best deal right, if she doesn't make the call now the deal's not gonna be done right, and that would mean it's gonna take weeks to get anofer one, so your client is just gonna to have to wait right."

"Sir let me ask you this, what is more important?" I said, leaning closer so other guides can't hear me. "The conception of a superior being that will save mankind, or a car she can obtain any time of the year?"

"*That* is the vessel of a superior being?" he asked sarcastically, pointing to Kym who is now flicking through a magazine and not daring to look in the mirror at her new hairdo, "now I've 'eard it all," he chuckled.

"Will you keep it down!" I hissed, "it's classified information. Now if you would be so kind as to direct your client back to mine then we will be out of your way to deal with your small problem of buying a car which I'm sure doesn't take much guidance at all."

Oh god, me and my mouth.

"Is that fighting talk?" he replied in a challenging tone.

"I'm just saying if you knew half of the intensity of this mission I'm on then you would, without hesitation, tell your client to finish my client's hair."

"Well if you only knew the lengths I went through to get the Lexus I.S 250 for my client, you'd be shuttin' your mouth," he said, pointing his finger in an intimidating way.

Wouldn't be surprised if the reason he came to be with us is because he died in a street brawl.

"A Lexus? You're valuing a car over the saviour of mankind?"

"I fink you're full of shit," he said leaning in closer, "my client is dealing with 'er car and your poxy client will just have to wait to get 'er locks blown right!"

Okay there is only one way to deal with this, fight a punk at his own game.

"Outside. Now." I demanded, cracking my knuckles.

We don't really physically fight like you do on earth, we don't even touch each other, it's all just energy, a bit like reiki; wave our hands and the energy comes shooting out. You would feel it as a slight breeze or gust of wind, it's just a territorial thing; we have to fight amongst ourselves to claim our space, billions of spirits here on earth, not a lot of room up in the atmosphere.

No sooner do we push ourselves out into the fresh air and it's game on. Punk guy wastes no time in sending me flying into a bunch of workers milling outside an office door, such a typical street fighter move, he obviously didn't leave that behaviour behind when he passed over.

I quickly wrapped my energy around his neck region and watched as he stood there, tongue lolling out the side of his mouth, his eyes rolling back into his head. An earth woman who ran through him to catch her bus briefly obscured my view and I didn't see his hand raise up to put energy around my arm and flip me over on to the pavement. I think the neck move took a lot of my energy; as I rise to an upright position, the energy coming from me is really lagging.

Closing in on punk guy I put pressure onto him forcing him to also hit the pavement, swinging my energy from side to side at him. It appears only a few bursts are connecting, I really am off my fighting game today, maybe the illusion of time spell I put over Rebecca has taken a lot out of me.


I shouldn't use the word 'spell', it sounds dark and you cannot imagine the trouble I would be in if I used a spell for my personal agenda, forget the in-between, it would be straight to hell where my soul would cease to exist in a ball of ash. They are lenient up there and forgive a lot but there is a line.

Punk man has regained the advantage while I was off in my own thoughts and has thrown me against a parked car; lucky for the person who owns the Hyundai Getz, I weigh nothing otherwise he would be blaming someone for dinting his car and not leaving a note.

I am so out of energy and should just call time out, I mean I'm sure by now the hairdresser is off the phone to her car broker and Kym is almost finished, he has defended his territory and I have shown punk man that I will not back down from a challenge and that's what this little exercise is all about.

Signalling to punk man that I am defeated, he pulls me to my feet in a show of respect and we wander silently back into the salon. His client appears to be back in the shop with good news, as she is excitedly telling her co-worker about the car. I glance over to where Kym was sitting to see a vacant chair staring back at me, I frantically scan the salon but it appears she is gone. Made my way towards the front counter to ask the hairdresser where she went and then remembered she has no physical way of engaging in a conversation with me, so I exited with such speed that light wouldn't be able to keep up.

I'm only hoping that Kym had followed the trail of intuitive breadcrumbs I planted and is on her way to the beauty salon for a leg wax otherwise she is just a floating in a sea of diversions!

**Kym**

I didn't worry about the hairdresser drying my hair completely, she excused herself halfway through to make an urgent call and it took me a while to look in the mirror to see the results, mainly because I was frightened at what I may see, but once I got up the courage, I was rather pleasantly surprised so I didn't bother staying for her to finish it off. It looked brilliant the way it sat, not straight and lifeless but bouncy and full of life, even my face looks different. So I paid the bill and left; there was a slight breeze as I exited the salon, and the way my new hairstyle dances around my face makes me feel as free as a bird.

I quickly crossed the street not really knowing where I was going, for some strange reason I felt like I just wanted to walk around for a while. I hadn't forgotten about the girls back at the shop frantically packing orchids for the one and only big order I am ever likely to receive, seems strange that everything is happening in one day. As I walked past a coffee cart the pleasant aroma of coffee catches my attention.

I have never drank coffee before, caffeine is an addictive substance, so I have always stuck with my herbal tea. That's what my mother always used to drink too, there was never any coffee in the house so I guess I just stuck with the devil you know.

Mandy drinks it by the gallon but understandable with the workload she has to deal with. But today I'm trying new things, and a double shot latte or a macchiato both sound interesting, very modern. I stood blushing at the coffee cart for a while figuring out what to have but first I'd better call the shop and let them know where I am and check to see if things are going well. If it wasn't such an unusually busy day I would take the day off.

I found a phone box and dialled the shop number; it's such a splendid day, one of those macchiato things by the water fountain in the square would be a delightful way to spend time before going to work. Mandy picked up and I explained I had managed to squeeze myself in for a haircut at the salon and thanked her for leaving the number on my bathroom vanity. Mandy seemed a bit taken aback, quite understandable as Mandy has never known me to have a haircut and I can only imagine when this conversation ends she will be dying to tell someone that I had finally gone to a salon.

She was more taken aback when I told her I was just grabbing a quick takeaway coffee and I would be more than happy to order one for her. It was only then I remembered that darling little summer dress I had seen in the boutique store, and I made mention to Mandy about trying it on.

When she gained composure yet again, she assured me there was no need to worry too much about things at the shop as the orchids had come pre-packed in gel cups to keep them fresh.

The only thing her and Tamara have to do is pack them into the special boxes and put our label on them, and they were well ahead of time as the truck wasn't expected till around 1pm. It also helped that they had an extra pair of hands with Mandy's eldest child Elliot being off school today due to an exaggerated bout of the sniffles. In fact Mandy said they should have it all sorted soon. This is great news; it seems the order may not be as big of a deal as I first thought. Assuring Mandy that I would be in as soon as I nip past the boutique shop and her assuring me once again not to rush as everything is fine and to enjoy my time, I place the receiver back and proceed to make my way back to the coffee cart.

**Elizabeth**

This is bad.

I have just arrived at the boutique and Kym is nowhere to be seen. I was putting my hopes in the fact she'd follow the breadcrumbs, but it appears not and I cannot feel her energy anywhere; I desperately need to tune into her. But keeping Rebecca at bay and fighting the punk rocker has zapped all my remaining energy and it's going to take some time to rebuild it.

The good news is the blue summer dress I picked out for her is still here which means there is a slight chance she could come back.

I could zap to the florist shop in the hope she has just listened to her head and not her heart, gone back to her old habits and headed to work, but I cannot run the risk of Rebecca seeing me, Lizard and Gypsy are with the delivery man at the moment and I cannot even tune into where they are at. Man that energy block I put on Rebecca has really taken its toll but I don't have time to dwell on that, it's not going to last forever and it's already 10.25am earth time. Retracing the steps of the morning I planted into Kym's head, I decided the next stop would probably be the beauty shop.

**Kym**

I had to giggle slightly when I ordered my macchiato, which is a shot of coffee with whipped milk on top, the poor cart barista was totally exasperated after explaining the differences to me, but I'm sure he would have taken delight in explaining if he didn't have other orders, he seems very good at his craft.

I found a lovely park bench under the shade of a tree to sip my new-found drink and happily swung my legs out in front of me, soaking in the warmth of the day and enjoying the sensation of the coffee on my taste buds. I don't know why I have never indulged in the coffee experience before; it really does go to show how much of a rut I am in.

I glanced down at my legs under the hem of my beige pencil skirt and realised how much I have let myself go, the long black hairs were faint but noticeable enough; I cannot recall the last time I had my legs waxed. I think I tried waxing when I was back in my teens, since then I have just shaved if the razor happened to be in the shower but I think I threw the last razor out some time ago now. I may just get a wax right after I visit the boutique for the new summer dress I saw this morning. I'm sure Mandy won't mind; I cannot imagine a leg wax takes long, perhaps after I buy the dress I should call her again to see how things are going. Or do I need to get the legs done first, hmm; no I think it may be better to buy the dress first. After all on a glorious day like today it may get snapped up quite quickly.

### Elizabeth

Okay I'm really starting to panic.

She's not at the beauty salon either, although the appointment I had left free so when she walks in they would have a spot, has not been assigned so I guess the good news is that she hasn't been in yet.

Although I said that about the dress.

God I hope she is not using her brain, she could be anywhere!

I look to the heavens for a sign of where she could possibly be. Time is ticking and if I don't get her back to the shop within the hour Rebecca is going to realise she has been stuck in a time warp and there goes any hope of my promotion. I'm not regretting what I have done, one thing you learn up there is not to have regrets, use it as a stepping stone. If it works out good, then great; if not, well it's experience, but I am seriously realising that my initiative may cost a huge delay today.

I look around at the spirit guides around me going about their business not noticing one another.

I would start asking around if any of them had seen Kym but because I didn't take a proper look at her hairdo before she left the salon I have no idea if she still has long brown hair with straight ends, or now has short, highlighted hair, or bob style hair with pink tips.

I do know she was wearing that hideous beige pencil skirt, a cream coloured blouse tucked in and her Hush Puppies footwear, which makes me think after all the seeds I installed last night, including the dress and the hairy legs, she must be coming back here. If I wait she may turn up, but then again what if she doesn't.

Contemplating my dilemma I spied an old spirit sitting on the pole 100 paces from where I was standing. It was Larry, an old man who had passed over a billionth of a second before I did. We met at the pearly gates and then he got sent back to earth to draw attention to a body stuck under a stairwell as a result of an accident that happened when he was a teenager at an old church. Larry enlisted the help of a client on earth called Lisa Collins, who after much convincing, managed to lead police to the church. Don't know why he picked her; she was just as crazy as he was. I was just observing back then, I wasn't allowed to interfere. I learned when I first crossed over about spirits who were caught up in their own death situation and couldn't cross over properly until they right the wrong.

Larry was a homeless man who got kicked in the head by a horse when he was a child so he was a bit simple when he was on earth, but he was such a character. That's not what killed him though; actually I'm not sure what killed him.

And since completing his task of righting the wrong, Larry is now a freelancer and not assigned any clients, he just pops in and out whenever the situation requires him to. If he is sitting up a pole it means he hasn't any particular place he needs to be so now is my chance to call on help.

"Larry," I wave frantically as he spies me and starts to slide down the pole backwards in his tattered old jacket and holey boots. Larry is a spirit of few words so you have to keep it simple.

If I can get him to go to Kym's florist shop and report back while I wait here in case Kym turns up then that would work to my advantage as Rebecca wouldn't suspect Larry is there on business unless of course she asks him.


"Listen," I said when I caught up with him and explained the situation, "I need you to go to Kym's florist shop which is about 2,000 paces North West of where we are now, and see if there is a woman there wearing a beige skirt."

I'm pretty sure her friend Mandy was wearing purple this morning and I'm sure the other young girl there would not be wearing beige.

"Her name is Kym," I repeated slowly so he would understand.

"Kym not there," Larry said not moving from the spot and shoving his yellowed finger up his nose.

"Um, are you sure? You haven't looked?"

"Don't need to."

"Why not?"

"'Cos she's there."

He pointed his finger to a very distant Kym, sporting her new hairdo and wearing a new blue dress, walking towards the beauty store in a crowd of faces. The only thing letting her down was those Hush Puppies shoes.

"Oh thank god!" I screeched to the heavens and grabbed Larry for a joyous circle dance, "thank you, thank you."

Larry started to dance a jig as well nearly knocking me off my feet with his heavy boots. I could feel my energy getting stronger again as I danced around with Larry, and was about to go to Kym when Rebecca suddenly appeared in my line of vision throwing me off balance with her inflamed eyes.

"The illusion of time spell!" Rebecca screeched in an agitated but controlled manner, "you think you could trick me with a bubble of time?"

"Well, clearly I did," I said, recovering from her surprise appearance.

"Oh no you didn't," she said, "you are forgetting you're not the only one the witch doctor taught his tricks of the trade too. The only difference is he taught me how to recognise and undo them. You're not that smart Elizabeth."

"Well what choice did you give me Re-becca? You and your controlling ways; there is no room for improvement, just get the job done."

"Not to the risk of a mission!" Rebecca hissed, "any other mission, fine, but lots could have happened here. You could have now jeopardised this whole mission with your lame side-line field trips, how many times do I have to repeat myself; stop interfering!"

"Well guess what? I still have my client and I have improved on her and we still have heaps of time left until the male subject arrives, so I guess my little side-line field trips are not so lame after all Rebecca."

"So where is she then?" Rebecca asked, throwing her hands in the air in exasperation, "where is this new and improved Kym?"

"What do you mean? She is right over..."

Oh shit.

I frantically search the surrounding area for her but she's disappeared again.

"So where is she?" Rebecca said, sounding alarmed now, "you better know where she is."

"Pfft she had an appointment with the beautician," I scoffed, "she will be inside getting her legs done, I'll go get her and meet you back at the shop okay."

I quickly turn and push my way through the wall to the waxing shop hoping Rebecca doesn't follow me, I can feel her glare bore into the back of my head and I know she is dying to say 'I told you so'. I get inside and scan the shop quickly but I cannot feel Kym's energy, in fact I have a feeling she is nowhere near this facility.

And it's no wonder; the appointment I had reserved for her has been taken by another smug guide that passed away from what appears to be severe obesity and is now sitting beside her client as she gets her facial hair waxed.

Damn I only took my eye off the ball for a second; as I said it's a dog-eats-dog world in the spirit kingdom.

I suddenly feel Kym's energy again, and I can also feel that Larry is with her.

Oh no.

"So is she here?" Rebecca said appearing beside me. Rebecca knows damn well she's not and is waiting for me to admit I have lost the client.

"Correction, you have lost the client *again*!" said Rebecca reading my mind and unable to restrain herself from waiting for me to admit it.

"I haven't lost her," I snapped trying to block Rebecca out so I can tune into Kym's energy. On a busy street like this with so many energies around, it's near impossible to pin her down.

"Well I hope not," Rebecca said, sounding panicked, pulling out her clipboard, "it's now 11.40am earth time, we have to get her back to the shop now!"

"Okay don't panic," I said, "I'll just try and tune into Larry."

Spirits are easier to find than physical humans.

"Larry?" Rebecca asks.

"Yes Larry, that's who's with Kym," I said tuning in, "ha found them, they are 1100 paces from here and I have a feeling Larry is leading her back to the shop."

"It better not be the Larry I'm thinking of," said Rebecca gripping my arm without touching me. "Elizabeth, it better not be Larry the freelance spirit," she said, her eyes burning in fury again.

There is no point denying it, she already knows it's *that* Larry, she already knows what happens when you leave your client unattended and Larry gets a hold of him or her, Larry loves practical jokes, so it's best I get there as quickly as possible.

"They're not far from here," I said to Rebecca, trying to smooth it over as I hurry in the direction of Larry's energy.

"Elizabeth I swear when this is over I will be putting you on report."

I spied Larry and Kym, Kym is strolling down the street looking fabulous with her new dress, new hairdo, and what appear to be new shoes.

She has ditched those Hush Puppies for some strappy sandals. Larry is strolling beside her wearing a top hat and carrying a cane as he walks proudly along in his tattered clothes. Kym looks amazing, if the urgency wasn't there to get her back to the shop right now I would have a wee proud moment to myself.

I pull my feet off the gravity field to get to them, I have a feeling Rebecca is behind me and has done the same; as I fly through the air, Larry spots me, and the all-too-familiar glint of mischief flashes in his eyes.

# 4

## Cameron

Yeah well I am sitting at home basically with my finger up my you-know-what, waiting to start work after the boss told me that because I have to cart a truck load of pansies up north I'd better start later, which was fine because a bloke needs a sleep-in after spending years getting up at the crack of dawn. But the bloody trouble is when you're used to getting up with the noisy fucking birds; your body tends to wake up at the same time regardless of what you are doing, so here I was, wandering around the house with Eliah and Jay-Jay wondering what a bloke should do on a morning off.

When you have the whole day off it's different, you can plan to do shit, but when you have the morning off, then there is no fucking point starting anything, you may as well be at fucking work. It's not like a bloke can go down the pub and have a couple of cold ones before jumping in the driver's seat, it's bloody pathetic. And to make matters worse they have taken my 30 tonne rig off me and swapped it for this half-pint 5 tonne thing. The boss reassures me it will give them a chance to service my truck while I'm on this delivery. Bullshit.

I still don't know why I was taken off my normal delivery of a load of frozen meat for a load of fucking flowers anyway, especially when I have to drive overnight to get them there.

Better not be the start of a new venture the boss is getting into 'cos I'd be telling him right now there is no way I'd be doing this all the time, especially in a poxy little truck like the one they have given me to do this job.

Luckily I can leave enough food out for the cats for overnight, but if it becomes a regular thing then I'm going to have to find someone to look after them or tell work to shove it. I mean what's the point of having pets if I'm not around; anyway Eliah and Jay-Jay are more than just pets, they're like my kids and it's not like you can just leave ya kids on their own for weeks on end, so yeah if this is the start of carting flowers over a state line then I'll be looking for a new job.

So still walking around the house wondering what one does on a useless waste of a morning off when I get a call to say the flowers that I was waiting to pick up are ready now, I was meant to pick them up at 1pm, or thereabouts.

I appreciate the gesture of calling me earlier and all but it doesn't really put me at an advantage time-wise as the lunch time traffic around the CBD where this bloody florist shop is, is going to be a fucking nightmare.

But what's a bloke to do? I figured I could wait around here for another hour being bored shitless or make tracks early and get this shit over and done with. Legally my logbook's all square so I'm in my truck on the way to the florist shop to pick up pansies for some pansy show up north, just fucking lovely!

**Kym**

This day seems to be getting better and better. I had just ducked in a payphone box to call Mandy again to let her know I'm on my way in now after a couple of distractions and it turns out the order is all packed, the sales docket is all printed and put into the computer, and apparently the truck is on its way to pick them up.

This is amazing, I don't even feel the need to rush into the shop and make sure it's all right; not that I ever doubted Mandy's ability to pull something like this off as she has great management skills, but I like to be in control and know what is going on, not being there today of all days is a bit out of character for me.

Mandy I think, is more surprised to learn I have been buying shoes and dresses, so she didn't mind at all that I wasn't in the shop on the day my little shop has made up the biggest order yet. She said I deserved a day off and I should take it, even though she has begged me to call past so she can see my new look which she expressed great excitement about.

I declined her kind offer of a day off as I really do have to call into the shop and do the displays but now the urgency has gone. Well to be honest I never felt the urgency today, it was like my fairy godmother came and sprinkled fairy dust on me in the night.

I feel like a princess in this new dress, I love the way it flows around my legs, it's not even bothering me that I never got round to getting my legs waxed.

I couldn't get into the beautician that was close to the dress shop as there was a rather large lady there hesitating at the reception. She seemed to have a bit of a problem with facial hair; the poor woman looked so embarrassed to be there. She seemed reluctant to commit and there was only one open appointment left, the chick behind the counter was rather impatient waiting for the large lady to make up her mind so she waved me in instead.

So I told her I won't be taking the appointment, after all my legs were not that bad compared to her face and I have stockings on, so I left. But when I did look down, I realised the lovely loafers, as comfortable as they are, certainly look ridiculous with my new summer dress so I decided to treat myself to a new pair of shoes instead.

I hang up the phone and go to step out of the phone box.
The door seems to be stuck.
I push gracefully so as not to be noticed by passers-by. I have slight panic starting to loom. It happens with me, I go into a panic rather quickly if I'm stuck or enclosed; I think I may be slightly claustrophobic.

When the door didn't move I tried pulling it towards me but it only moved enough to let a small mouse through. I pushed again but this time with a little bit of force but still it's like something is leaning against it. Okay I'm just going to have to breathe and try and calm myself down as panic is definitely rising. I'm only hoping that it's a phone box that has a new safety feature installed and there is a timing mechanism on here, a bit like those new modern public loos that are around now, but I don't see any buttons for a door release.

I could always call Mandy and get her to send someone but I don't even know where I am, I'll just have to keep trying the door. I don't really want to draw attention to myself in case the door isn't stuck and it's some kind of modern thing that I haven't caught up with yet. How embarrassing would that be.

So I'll keep trying the door and concentrate on calming myself down as my anxiety is building and I do not want to have a panic attack in a phone booth where everyone can see me.

### Elizabeth

Bloody Larry.

My client is in a phone booth and Larry is holding the door shut.

Just as I got to her, Kym ducked into the phone booth and shut the door behind her, causing me to go crashing into the side, followed by Rebecca crashing into me. Don't get me wrong, we can walk through walls but only if we are grounded, if we aren't connected, just free floating, then we are just like everyone else, we crash on impact. The difference is we can't get hurt; apart from our pride.

It's not exactly black and white; we have feelings but don't feel, we have accidents but don't get hurt, and we can also walk through solid objects but not fly through them. It was easier being a human sometimes, at least you knew what to expect.

But anyway Rebecca's pride is damaged, not to mention her pressure gauge is about to blow. Larry thought it was absolutely hilarious I crashed as I wanted to take back my client and guide her to the florist shop.

Larry pushes himself up against the phone booth door and starts kicking his legs in the air so neither Rebecca nor I can get near him to pull him off, physically or telepathically.

I tried going into the phone booth through the side and coaxing Kym out that way and managed to get inside once I was grounded, but with Larry spreading his spiritual weight around to weigh that of an elephant, it's really hard to get Kym to push the door open. Bloody Larry, he thinks it's so funny.

Kym has now turned into a fidgeting lunatic as I'm trying with all my haste to get Larry to move away and let her out. I went back out and managed to get though his kicking legs but now he had one foot pressed on my face as I have him by the arms pulling him off the door, I cannot see Kym's face but I can feel her panic.

I'm trying to calm her down by sending as much calming light as possible but when you have an old homeless drunken spirit insisting he shove his toe up your nose, it's hard to do. Not that the calming light would work anyway, well not on Kym. It's almost impossible to do, some have success, especially when you are facing a life and death situation, like being stuck in the mountains with a broken leg and knowing that you may not make it out alive if help doesn't arrive soon. Normally people who have been rescued in these situations talk about an inner calm they suddenly feel and it helps them think more clearly and then they're able to save themselves until help arrives, yeah well that's us, we can take the credit for it; but people like Kym who have suffered a trauma in their past life (she was buried alive back in the 1600s) automatically bring that fear into this life when caught in a situation that feels similar, so no amount of calming light is going to calm her fear of being stuck in a phone booth until I can move Larry from the door.

"What is taking so long?" Rebecca hissed in panic.

I wish I could send her calming light as *her* panic levels are not helping *my* panic levels.

"Oh nothing much, maybe it's just this 1 tonne spirit holding the door," I said sarcastically as I continued to pull at Larry's arm to move him. "You could help Rebecca."

Rebecca throws the clipboard to the ground causing a passer-by to trip up and look back in astonishment at what they tripped on, they will probably write a letter to the council for uneven footpaths, happens all the time.

I get behind Larry's shoulder and we push with all our might. Larry is loving every minute of this and is singing some song that he learnt off a Caribbean pirate as we are pushing him; and poor Kym is now pale with anxiety as she pushes at the door. This is not good and I'm thinking I may have to put it to Rebecca that she calls in Bossman to get Larry removed by reporting him as a hazard to the mission when Lizard appears, causing me to jump backwards at the shock of his bold presence.

I land up against a pole upside down and Larry is now positively shaking with frantic laughter.

"We've got a problem, we've got a big problem!" said Lizard in hysterics.

"What now?" sighs Rebecca, dusting herself off and picking her clipboard up.

"The truck driver... he has arrived at the shop, like now, he's there now!" Lizard panted.

Oh shit.

"Well then stall him!" shrieked Rebecca, "don't let him leave, this mission will not fail. I don't care what you do; just don't let him leave till we get there."

"Okay got it... I think," Lizard said, about to get himself back to the shop.

"No, wait!" Rebecca screamed, "help us get Kym out first."

Lizard now looks even more panicked as he starts shaking in a frantic way.

"What's your problem?" Rebecca screams at him, "get Larry out of the way!"

"I don't know what you want me to do," Lizard said as he starts to sob uncontrollably.

"Just remove this clown!" Rebecca yelled.

"I thought you wanted me to stall Cameron," Lizard said, totally confused.

"Oh this is a joke," Rebecca said, suddenly calm. Her mood-swings are off the planet, well technically, they actually are.

"Get the subject out of the phone box," Rebecca said in a scary calm tone worse than yelling.

I'm still upside down but I glance at Kym who is now pushing really hard at the door and is trying hard to fight back tears. Shit if Lizard opens the door now then...

"No, wait!" I cry, but it's too late.

In one swift desperate move Lizard pulls Larry from the door, Larry may have blown himself up to the weight of an elephant but Lizard weighs 10 times that. Man why didn't I think of this at the beginning, so many energies in the city scrambles the brain.

Larry goes flying through the air and Kym spills out onto the street with force, crashing to the ground and landing awkwardly, crying in pain as she hits the pavement.

Oh no!

"What the hell?!" I started at Lizard, "tell me you couldn't foresee that coming! Didn't you think that pulling the weight off the door suddenly would cause my client who was pushing hard from the inside to thrust through the door when the weight was removed?"

What am I talking about, of course he wouldn't know about push/pull forces etc, he is from the dinosaur era.

"Well you told me to get rid of him, I-I- got flustered," Lizard exclaimed, even more confused.

"Never mind," Rebecca hissed, "just get Kym back to the shop. Lizard, go and stall that truck driver. I'll go and stall that bus so we can get her there quicker, go, go, go!"

I don't think Rebecca has realised that Kym has hurt her ankle, and quite badly, I think a taxi would be much better.

Rebecca and her clipboard disappear into the busy street and Lizard does the same, leaving a sudden gust of wind blowing across the pavement causing ladies to suddenly hold their skirts down. I straighten up to go to Kym's rescue. But she is not at the spot she had landed at all. I zone into her energy just as I spot a young gentleman helping her into a taxi.

Kym is hobbling on her ankle and the strap of her new shoe lies broken in the street. Kym is looking at this gentleman as if he is her knight in shining armour; well actually I know she is thinking just that because I can read her thoughts. The young man's guide is there; a hopeless romantic military personnel from Napoleon's era of 1805. You know those French types.

So of course he thinks his client's encounter with this damsel in distress is right up his alley as he thinks he is a bit of a hero to the ladies, but I suppose with all the battles going on in his day and the amount of woman and children he saved I guess he has earned it.

But not today and not on my watch. Oh my god, why of all days did we have a hero show up just as Kym hurts her ankle, right at the moment she is meant to be meeting her future love, why!?

I fly towards the taxi trying to catch it before it leaves; at least she is in transport already so I guess I could thank this young man for doing part of my job. I went to jump in the taxi with Kym when I got overshadowed by Mr French Napoleon guide.

"Stop right there," he ordered in a commanding voice that he hasn't lost since he died a noble death in the battle of Rivoli. "There is a lady in need of medical assistance, please step back from the moving carriage," he continued as his young man gets into the taxi with Kym. Oh no, Kym is smitten by him.

"I'm Elizabeth, this is my client," I said to Napoleon man as he holds his hand up to block me from getting into the taxi.

"I found your client in dire need of assistance and unattended. She needs urgent medical attention so if you would like to step back while we attend to her that is an order from a military officer."

"She doesn't need medical assistance," I argued, "she needs to get back to her florist shop as she is about to encounter a major event that has been placed in her path."

"Well I suggest ma'am, that you delay that until the lady is attended to."

I cannot argue with this noble-man any more, sure his intentions for his client are all well and good but this is an emergency.

"No, I cannot delay," I told him, as I step around him, "this is a matter of the High Council," I said.

I'm not normally one to disobey a figure of authority but I have no choice as an even bigger authority, as in the big, big cheese of the universe is counting on me to get one subject from Point A to Point B and Kym is now in a taxi with a charming young fellow sporting a sprained ankle. My senses felt a strong energy coming from behind me but I wasn't quick enough, Larry whooshes past me at jet speed and lands in the taxi beside Kym, the taxi roars off and Larry glances back at my horrified expression, grinning his toothless grin and waving back at me looking like a cat amongst the pigeons.

## 5

### Kym

So now I'm in a taxi with a beautiful young man who has the most mesmerising eyes, on my way to the emergency department after I fell out of the phone booth and twisted my ankle.

So much for my new modern shoes, I'm sure if I was still in my brown loafers this wouldn't have happened.

The door of the phone booth was jammed so much I started to imagine all sorts of things like dying in there. The intense knot in my throat was tightening and I obviously didn't know my own strength as I more frantically started pushing at the door with brute force. All of a sudden the door loosened and I flew out, landing sideways on the pavement with my new shoes breaking as my ankle turned the opposite direction to my leg.

I was feeling like a bit of a wally and just hoping my new free-flowing dress wasn't up around my head when suddenly this young man appears by my side and asks if I'm okay. I tried to play down my pain but I just couldn't, it was intense. He was lovely and insisted he accompany me to the accident department to get it checked out.

So here I am in a taxi.

My ankle hurts really badly, but I'm trying not to let it show. I'm starting to think that having my hair done and buying a new dress and shoes was not such a good idea, I should have just gone to work like I always do and this wouldn't have happened! I guess if my ankle is broken then having crutches may not hinder me too much at the shop, I might just have to get Mandy to help me out a bit more. Not that she hasn't done enough already today. But I shouldn't jump to too many conclusions as it may just be a twist.

Part of me wants to cry and feel the comfort of this lovely young gentleman beside me and another part of me has the urge to tell the taxi driver the wrong directions and have him drive around for hours in confusion just to have a bit of a laugh. Oh dear, I hope this sudden split in thoughts isn't a result of a concussion.

**Cameron**

So this is just fucking lovely.

After fighting traffic through the CBD I finally get here after missing it a couple of times and driving around the block 'cos I expected a bigger florist shop, I mean the way the boss was carrying on, it was like I was to collect gold flowers for the queen, but turns out it's only a small shop wedged between a café and a video store. I do vaguely remember seeing the place on my rare trips to town; probably noticed it so I knew to avoid it considering I think they used to also sell birds there.

I was fucking hoping they still didn't, hate the feathered things. But once inside I was relieved as there didn't seem to be one bird in sight. I was a bit surprised how small it was, couldn't swing a small dog in there if you tried, there was no loading bay or space round back, so I had to double park outside causing the ponsey café owner next door to really make my day and tell me I can't park there as not only was it a bus lane, I was blocking his precious customers from seeing the café.

I felt like telling him his customers would probably prefer if they didn't see the café as the décor is fucking ugly, but anyway after arguing with the git for a couple of minutes about parking spaces and fucking lack of, I proceeded to load the less than 20kg weight boxes that took up only a quarter of my truck space, by hand I may add.

I wished I had my normal truck then I really would show that git next door what blocking someone's view was about.

I thought it was some sort of joke to begin with, I mean a courier van could have done the same fucking job, but because the lady in the florist shop was expecting me and the paperwork was all up to scratch and ready to go, I reneged on calling the boss and asking if he was on drugs.

The lady at the shop told me she wasn't the owner and hoped everything was in order when she handed me the paperwork. I smiled back at her with the politeness the boss expects from his slaves but I really wanted to tell her I don't give a rats-arse who owns the shop, just as long as you don't give me the wrong paperwork.

So after expecting a truck load of boxes and getting them in there and realising the truck is still three quarters empty, I'm filling out the paperwork wondering what the fuck, when a fucking bus proceeds to break down in front of me and blocks my exit.

This is great, this is just fucking great!

**Kym**

I am so out of my comfort zone right now.

We arrived at the hospital, and Nathanial, my young rescuer, is sitting here with me as we are waiting on the results of my x-ray.

I was seen to rather quickly by the doctors on call which is great considering since our arrival things went a bit haywire; an unattended wheelchair mustn't have had its brake applied as it rolled down the corridor crashing into the cleaning trolley; and a lady behind a curtain just had her catheter mysteriously empty all over the floor causing one of the nurses to slide in it and lose her balance.

But that's not why I am out of my comfort zone.

You see ever since I can remember, I have never touched the ground with my bare feet, I cannot bear the thought of my skin touching where others have walked, even with my new sandals I kept my skin-coloured stockings on, probably what caused my foot to slide in them and the strap to break. It's not some type of phobia or anything like that it's just that I have never been outside my flat without covering my feet. Even inside my house I always wear slippers or aqua sandals in the shower.

And unfortunately Nathanial insisted I take my remaining sandal off in case I need to hobble, as he doesn't want me to topple off it.

And he also took the stocking off my foot. So I am sitting on the edge of the bed and so far my feet have not touched the ground but I cannot help but stare at my feet, naked and bare, just flopping around, it doesn't feel right. In fact I feel exposed, I didn't even keep the clothes I walked out the door in this morning. In a moment of temporary madness I insisted the sales woman at the boutique where I brought the dress throw them out.

Sensing my anxiety Nathanial asked if I'm okay, he is so sweet and there are a million emotions going on with me at the moment. Not knowing what to say to that beautiful, concerned face, I told him I was cold. As he wraps his jumper around my shoulders, I amazingly strike up a conversation with him. We kinda had a bit of small talk going on in the taxi but I was more concerned, not only with my ankle, but with the fact I wanted to give him what Mandy's kids refer to as a 'wet willy'; sticking my wet finger in his ear, it was such an over-whelming sensation that I had to sit on my hands to prevent myself from doing this, I mean imagine if I did.

He would have thought I was some kind of nut and perhaps was taking me to the wrong hospital. The same urge made me really concentrate on not telling the taxi driver to take a wrong turn; the urge to do this did pass. So I am only hoping it is a temporary concussion and all is fine again.

Anyway I have found out that our Nathanial is in college studying human rights and ancient history and that he is fascinated with the French revolution; if I wasn't in so much pain I would pay more attention as he is rather interesting. I told him when I was working as a librarian I was often found engrossed in the history section when I should have been shelving books in the romance section, which he found amusing.

He's insisted he stay with me as he assures me he is not missing a lecture. I don't think my ankle is broken, as I can move my foot so I am just hoping I can go home soon.

I rang Mandy from Nathanial's cell phone just to let her know where I was. She said she would offer to come and get me but apparently the truck driver that picked up the flowers is having a bit of an altercation with a bus driver outside the shop so Mandy said it may be best to stay behind in case it gets out of control, seems a bit scary, so may be a good thing I'm not there.

**Cameron**

I've just about had enough of this bus driver. I am ready to punch his lights out if he tells me to be patient one more time; he has a strong accent which is not helping with this communication breakdown. Well, when it suits him. Either that or he has a common case of selective hearing; as he doesn't understand when I tell him I am running late and have a load of fucking flowers to get to mid-state by tomorrow, but does understand when I tell him what a timewaster he is.

The bus seems to be idling perfectly fine to me so cannot see what the problem is but the driver is claiming it will not move forward when he plants his foot on the accelerator, it just wheel spins and the engine revs like it wants to move forward but cannot.
And yes, turns out this is true as I stood and witnessed it.

So after watching this wannabe driver have several attempts at trying to make his bus go forward and my patience slightly unsettling as clearly it does not want to go forward,

I knocked on the bus door and offered to release his handbrake for him and maybe put it in gear properly because that's what it sounds like to me, and now the bus driver is accusing me of criticising his driving, which he would be correct in saying.

I mean for fucks sake if the thing isn't going forward after 3 attempts then get out of the fucking thing and find out what is wrong, but he reckons he can't do that as it is regulations and he has to stay in the bus at all times when passengers are involved.

Of course I had to inform him that I feel that is the biggest load of bullshit to come out of anyone's mouth, so he proceeded to quote some regulation sub section blah, blah. All off the top of his head which really confirmed to me he is not a real driver 'cos real drivers don't give a shit about the rules; so we had a little altercation, not physical, just verbal. And some of the passengers were a little concerned so he put the fucking bus on lockdown until the police turn up.

Thank christ I had my logbook all squared up, not that my logbook would save me if that git reported me as some sort of terrorist that is trying to interfere with his bus.

So anyway I get a few brief reassuring words by the police about how they will move the bus as soon as possible and it's best I wait in the truck until the passengers are unloaded into a new bus that has just turned up.

And just as I was about to step back in my truck and wait until the circus act was over the bus suddenly jolts forward and ploughs into a stationary van in front.

So now they are waiting for a fucking tow truck.

If I wasn't so pissed off it would have been funny.

But I don't give a shit about that because I'm now nearly an hour late, so with the bus moved slightly forward I was able to manoeuvre my truck back far enough to squeeze past him, unfortunately I didn't see the ponsey café owner's flower pot, which was inconveniently placed in my blind spot on the footpath, and I ran over it.

I swear that was a set-up because I'm sure flower pots aren't allowed on the footpath, I mean come-on we live in an age where bus drivers are not allowed to get out of their fucking buses when carrying passengers!

If the police weren't there taking reports of what now appears to be a fucking bus accident, I would have just driven off, not giving a rats-arse about a flower pot as this truck doesn't have the company logo on it.

But since I have already drawn attention to myself I had to get out of the truck and exchange details with the twit-faced café owner who will make me replace the broken glazed flower pot and reckons it was there the whole time which I'm sure is a load of shit.

So now I'm really fucking late, over an hour and a half, I swear if anything else goes wrong on this trip, I'm gonna lose it.

# 6
## Operation KymCam Day 2

### Elizabeth

Rebecca is furious. No Rebecca is beyond furious; in fact Rebecca is now starting to burn red she is that stressed. Not a good time to tell her it suits her either.

Mind you I'm not far behind her. This day hasn't been a good one.

By the time I tracked Kym down again she had already left the hospital. I gave chase by air after Larry hijacked the taxi that was carrying Kym and her young nobleman, but the sound of Rebecca on my tail screaming profanities at me because I'd let Kym loose with Larry once again caused me to lose concentration and I lost sight of them when I tumbled under a low bridge.

Larry, who was watching me from the back of the speeding taxi, thought it was hilarious as he always does, and when the taxi veered left instead of right, which I had predicted, the energy faded and it took time to tune in again to find out which hospital Kym was at.

Didn't help that Larry interfered by scattering signals from Kym so I wouldn't know where to look.

Anyway, I decided to go to the nearest hospital and start searching. It wasn't hard, by the time I got to the second one and found a nurse sporting a bruised tailbone, patients traumatised, and the cleaner mopping up gold liquid on the floor; I knew Kym had to be here as the path of Larry's destruction was obvious. But it was too late, her ankle had been attended to and she was back at her apartment.

But now I have an even bigger problem.

"Okay," exhaled Rebecca through her red tinged nose, "what in the name of all Satan was that?!"

There she goes again, a mountain out of a molehill, yes it was a bad day but it wasn't exactly a Satan day; a Satan day is a hell beyond hell, volcano explodes sending lava kind of day; well, you get the picture.

Yesterday was just a big misunderstanding of time.

It's the morning after and we're all gathered in Kym's florist's shop licking our wounds at the mishaps yesterday. Lizard has strained his back trying to hold the bus to block Cameron's truck; and he was succeeding until his back gave way and the bus ploughed into a parked vehicle, running him over in the process. Luckily he has five afterlifes left.

Reptile man is that ancient he is losing his spiritual strength, he is coming into his 20 millionth year, so to hold the bus as long as he did, he did well.

We do have a second chance up here, we just come back as another reincarnation, not necessarily a human spirit like I am now, we could be flower, tree, insect, you name it. Everything recycles, and thank god, because if we just stayed as spirits we would have no survival and nothing to survive on, it's not just on earth that it's getting overpopulated, it's the same in the spirit world.

We didn't bother pursuing anything more or trying to change the course of action as Cameron had already gone with the load of flowers and is now one thousand and fifty kilometres away from Kym.

Kym spent the evening sharing a glass of wine with Mandy, her first glass of wine since a colleagues wedding 12 years earlier, sharing her excitement and bewilderment about her day and her meeting with her young nobleman; and me, well I spent the evening in Kym's apartment trying to lock Larry in a closet as he has taken a liking to Kym and decided to stick around.

I have worked out he is trying to alter her behaviour to more of a practical joker Kym.

I can see why he wants to do it as she has never come out of her shell and that joker side of Kym is programmed into her since birth, it just hasn't surfaced yet. But Larry's idea of a good time will not score points in popularity. Poor Kym, if she only knew what Larry had done with her sanitary pads.

Or what he fed her ring-neck parrot.


Rebecca hasn't reported back to Bossman yet about the 'delay'. I don't know where she spent the remaining time until now but the colour she was this morning, I would have said, in a state of despair.

Rebecca is waiting for me to answer because her question is not a rhetorical one, it's aimed at me.

"Things were going fine," I started, "but as you know Rebecca, we had some outside interference from another spirit."

"So is that the official report I have to give to Bossman?" she scolded, "or shall I just tell him the interfering spirit was you; which resulted in the injury of our female client?"

"It's just a sprained ankle," I mumbled, trying to play it down.

"Well if you want my opinion..." said Gypsy folding her hands behind her head and leaning back on her invisible chair not giving a care in the universe.

"You!" Rebecca screamed at Gyspy, causing everyone to jump with her booming voice, "where were you? I did not witness you once partaking in this mission."

"I was organising the flower pots," she sniffed, "someone had to, it, it, was a disgraceful display..." she trailed off.

"It was just the one flower pot Gypsy and it didn't even belong to this shop," said Lizard, disgusted at the injustice of the lack of effort on Gypsy's part and trying to score points with Rebecca, "the rest of the time I found you dozing next to our female client's Grandmother."

"I was not dozing, I was meditating and it's all in the name of this mission. I will not put up with these accusations," Gypsy said.

That was enough for Lizard to flash his rage colours and between Rebecca's red aura and Lizard's flashing colours it's like an electrical light show in here, you know those prisms you people buy and hang in the window to reflect light and make rainbow colours around the room? Yeah well, you have been conned, it doesn't come from the sunlight's reflection, chances are your spirit guides are having a tiff.

The argument going on between Gypsy and Lizard has given me time to collect myself, I don't know what else to say to Rebecca or Bossman for that matter, if she reports back. Yes I have to admit getting Larry involved was probably the downfall of this mission so far, I guess I didn't think in my panic to find Kym after she gallivanted off.

I forgot about Larry's reputation of stealing your clients and taking them on joyous rides. But the good news is we still have 11 days earth time, so the only reason Rebecca is in despair is because she wanted this mission done yesterday, without a hitch.

"Okay," Rebecca said, calmly easing herself back into a chair after sorting out the petty argument between Lizard and Gypsy, "let's just fix this shall we?" she said, opening her notebook up. "So first thing's first, where is the male client at present?"
Phew, that means for now she is not going to persist in analysing my actions of yesterday.
"450 clicks this side of the state line," Gypsy said, chewing on her invisible gum.
"And when is he due back from that delivery?" asked Rebecca.
"The time after the earth rotates away from the sun," said Lizard.
"So some time this evening?" Rebecca said, writing notes in her book, "and the female client, where is her present self?"

Rebecca knows where she is. She is just trying to make this meeting official and cross all her t's and dots her i's just in case she does have to report back to Bossman and the council; at least she can say she ran a 'professional' mission.

"She is in her usual habitat," I sighed while Rebecca continued to write in her minute book.

"… and the spirit that is Larry?" Rebecca asked in a patronising tone, pausing briefly from her scribbling to look at me, "is he going to give us any more trouble?"

I stare at her for a few seconds as she stares back at me in a Mexican glare-off moment, I'm throwing images up of me pushing Larry into a closet and locking it and trying to keep him from influencing my client in the hope I can divert Rebecca from seeing what is really going on behind the scenes

"No," I smiled at her, "Larry will not be jeopardising this mission."

"Good," she smirks back. "Okay then, we have work to do. We need to unite these two clients and I want this done by the time day turns back into night.

Yesterday's planned meeting failed miserably due to one client being delayed and one client being present earlier than expected; and yes reptile man I am aware that Gypsy helped in the packing of the flowers which resulted in the order getting done sooner."

"What?" Gypsy scoffed as Lizard slowly lowers his raised hand, "I like flowers, so sue me!"

"So I want Kym back here and I want Cameron back here and I want them back here at the same time," Rebecca scolded "I don't care how and I don't care what they are wearing."

Yip she is going to use that against me for the rest of my days, I really do need to get this promotion, I don't know how much more I can take of her.

"And because of yesterday's mind games," Rebecca continued, also glancing at me, "we will also be carrying these."

Rebecca produces the iports; they are octagon shaped mirrors that display the illusion of a pyramid, designed to spy on you; which means she has been back up to headquarters as these are only available if you request them.

Basically they are two way radios with video screens linked to your energy auras, and by the looks of it she has already programmed them into ours, there is no hiding from these.

"So each of you will carry one and I want a report from you via these every time your client makes a move," Rebecca said, "no nonsense means no fail! So connect with your clients, get a plan of how this connection is going to work and report back to me, I shall be waiting."

Without a word we collect out iports and disappear in opposite directions.

I hold back a bit on my way back to Kym's apartment, drifting through the atmosphere in a vortex tunnel getting some alone time and trying to get some sort of action plan going. Now we have these iports, I am going to have to work extra smart and quick to divert Rebecca's attention away while I fix what is really going on.

I didn't see this one coming, but the conversation with Mandy and the look in Kym's eyes last night tell me that I cannot allow a path diversion; otherwise she and Cameron will not work out.

Damn, why did Larry have to interfere? With Kym's new-found confidence at changing things in her daily routine, she has set a passage and now wants to explore other areas of life. Which is fine, as it is part of growth, and sometimes we do allow people to go off their planned path a little just to have an experience they may not get to have in their life's path, but it takes work to guide them back to their purpose and I don't have time for that.

Maybe another time with another client but I cannot run the risk of Kym and Cameron not meeting again. Which is a shame as Kym is glowing with happiness and it only took one day. Imagine what I could do with two days.

## Kym

Mandy is always talking about how everything happens for a reason and how we are part of a much bigger plan set out for us before we were born. I never agreed with her theory as I have always believed things just happen because as humans we control this. But I have never expressed this to Mandy simply because through her hard times, she had to have faith in something.

So you can imagine Mandy's theory on yesterday's events. I say this as I roll my eyes but it is kind-of funny how my day started, and ended, for that matter.

My ankle is sore and my pride is dented from falling out of a phone box. I have ruined a pair of new sandals that on a normal day I wouldn't have looked twice at, and I missed packing up the biggest order my shop has ever done to go dress shopping and get a new hairdo. But despite all of that I am ecstatic because I would like to announce to the world that I have a date with a lovely young man who is almost half my age.

I cannot believe it; I feel like I am in a big dream and any moment now I'm going to wake up and find my life back the way it was the day before. After telling Mandy about my day, I did something I hadn't done since my colleagues wedding some years ago, I opened a bottle of wine to celebrate.

The bottle that was given to me one Christmas and now housed an inch of dust from so long in storage, but it was the cherry on the top of what turned out to be a bizarre day.

Nathanial, my young date, stayed behind for coffee after escorting me and my sprained ankle back to my little apartment behind Mandy's house.

I couldn't thank him enough for his kindness but he just said he couldn't leave someone as lovely as me to hobble on alone. He too is also a lover of birds and he and Harry, my ring-neck parrot, seemed to hit it off perfectly. I was having such a great conversation with him about all sorts of things that I didn't even hear Mandy enter my apartment and of course you could imagine the look on her face, it was apparent then that she wasn't going to leave until she heard the full story of my day, especially as the only man Mandy has ever seen in my apartment is a plumber when my sink was blocked up. Any man in my apartment, let alone a young or handsome one, was bound to raise questions.

So when I escorted Nathanial to the door and gave thanks once again for everything he has done, it was then he asked if I would be interested in meeting him for a coffee tomorrow as his university is not far from my shop. So that's what is happening tomorrow, 10.30am at the coffee cart near the phone booth where I hurt my ankle.

I'm so excited but so nervous at the same time.

I had rung Mandy again this morning after a restless night as I didn't sleep well. It played on my mind all night, what happens if it leads to the bedroom? Okay I haven't even had coffee with him yet so I suppose I am putting the cart before the horse but this is uncharted territory for me, and I'm not sure if I am supposed to read signs or is it expected when you date someone these days? I'm no virgin, I had that experience with a brief relationship with a man whom I had worked with at the library unfortunately, and embarrassed to say, whose wedding I attended when he decided that the woman that headed the book buying department of the library would make a better bride than I.

I have Nathanial's mobile phone number and was embarrassed when I couldn't give him mine because I didn't own one, he looked at me a bit shocked to begin with but the expression soon left his face when I gave him my home landline phone number instead, so I guess he realises how out of touch with things I am, not that I think he cares. He seems to find that fascinating about me; that I am single and have never travelled overseas, and the fact that I live in the city and have never been to a sushi bar, but the funniest thing is that when I am around him I feel the urge to play tricks on him.

For example when he handed me his phone number I had the urge to hand him a piece of paper with morse code writing on it just to see the look on his face, it's totally strange.

So after chewing Mandy's ear off and giggling like a school-girl while teasing Harry the parrot with a piece of cheese as he sat on my shoulder, her advice to me was to relax, enjoy his company and stop reading too much into it. Easy for her to say as she always seems to be at ease with men.

While attempting to dress, I am cursing the fact I should have bought more of those beautiful dresses I saw in the shop yesterday as I cannot wear the same dress as yesterday and everything else I own is sensible long-length garments in brown.

I'm trying to figure out if I can make my clothes look less like my old library days and shaking off the urge to go all out and wear my old high school formal dress that I kept for sentimental reasons and looks like something out of a Disney princess movie, when Mandy phones me again.

I think she is checking in to make sure I haven't gone completely bananas and maybe got a tattoo overnight given my recent behaviour. Turns out she called into my shop on the way to drop the kids at school to retrieve Elliot's school shoes left there yesterday and there was a message flashing on the shop phone.

And well, it turns out they didn't need the orchids as they doubled up on their order and they are completely sorry for any inconvenience they have caused but are sending them back with the same transport company.

Luckily they paid a deposit in advance so it covered my transport costs but unfortunately not the flowers, I'm only hoping insurance can cover it. Oh dear, what a complete and utter waste of time.

So I'd better get into the shop as I guess I have to round up buyers for 3000 orchids today, unless Tamara's uncle is willing to take them back.

But what would he do with 3000 orchids after he has picked them? Hmm, it seems a bit strange that they doubled up like that, especially when my little shop is twelve hundred kilometres away and we have had more of a slow growing season than them.

I really should ring up and complain, I mean really, it's so unheard of these days that flowers are sent back. They are a perishable product and it seems so irresponsible that they ordered from a supplier twelve hundred kilometres away; but the more I am getting worked up thinking about it, the more frustrated I am about my clothes.

And I don't know what happened in my closet but it looks like a tussle has gone on in here as I have clothes and scarves everywhere. I simply cannot go on a date with these heavy knitted clothes and only one dress.

There is only one thing for it, I am going to have to brave the shops again and buy another outfit.

This damn leg aid is not making life easy and I know Mandy will be back soon to help me get dressed and drive me to my shop so I am sure she will be up to stopping off downtown and helping me pick out an outfit or two.

Sighing and feeling useless I attempt to struggle into the summer dress I purchased yesterday while balancing on one foot. My brown loafer shoe is the only one I can wear on my good foot and is not going to complement it well, so maybe some of those flat shoes that Mandy wears may also have to be put on the shopping list. Not that it matters what I am going to have on my feet as I have a giant sock hiding my hospital standard ankle support, so nothing is going to complement that well.

I express my frustration on the lack of options from my wardrobe to Harry my ring-neck parrot as I go about my morning routine with a struggle, but he seems a little quiet this morning; normally he chatters away back to me as I fluff around in the morning but unlike Tweety and Sylvester my two yellow canary's, Harry seems a little off.

In fact… Harry seems drunk!

I quickly hobble over to his cage for a closer look, hearing the door open behind me as Mandy makes her appearance.

Harry seems unsteady on his perch and his eyes are glassy; it seems he cannot stay straight.

Instinctively I pick up his water dish to sniff the contents thinking how ridiculous it is that I'm even thinking that Harry would have any alcohol in his water or that alcohol is the problem full stop. But it does appear Harry water dish is filled with wine.

"We'll take him to the vet," Mandy said over my shoulder trying to contain the amusement on her face as I break down in absolute horror, screeching about the amount of wine he must have consumed. Was I that drunk last night I tipped the contents of my wine glass into Harry's dish? Is my head that far up in the clouds that I accidently did that instead of tipping it down the sink? I remember I didn't finish the last glass of wine as I felt I had a little too much, especially with my pain killers but I only had a glass or two, I'd hardly call that drunk anyway. I know it wasn't Mandy as she wouldn't do such a thing but up until now I believed that I wouldn't do such a thing either.

Mandy consoles me and reassures that Harry will be just fine as she gathers his cage and my belongings and shuffles my hysterical self toward the door. Tears are welling in my eyes and bewilderment overcomes me on how such a thing could happen as we make our way to the car to stop off at the vet before making our way to the shop.

**Cameron**

Well what a waste of fucking time that was.

It turns out when I got my freight up to its destination, the pricks didn't want it.

In normal circumstances I would have just unloaded it and drove away saying it's your fricken problem but as it turns out they had tried to divert me five hundred kilometres before the destination but because I own a useless piece of technology called a mobile phone that seems to all of a sudden have a mind of its own and apparently decided to switch itself off back up the highway, turns out it is now my fricken problem. Now on orders from the boss who also agreed what a fricken waste of time it was, I am instructed to take the load of pansies back to tiny pin-hole of a shop where I got them from.

Which is just fricken fantastic; because if that café owner comes at me again about parking near his precious caffeine infested shop I am not likely to hold back at running over more of his glazed pots.

Being sleep deprived and finding out you have driven a long way just to get your freight turned back is not a good combination for any bloke.

Okay, so why should I care, I'm getting paid regardless, so if the pansies turned out to be boomerangs then what should it matter to me. Well it doesn't, so new subject.

This trip has put a different perspective on life; maybe I shouldn't be so serious all the time. Guys at work are always telling me to take a chill pill, it's alright for them as most likely they are sucking on happy pills the way the carry on sometimes, but being an honest bloke, the truth is I haven't had anything to be happy about.

Never met the right woman, therefore never had kids, never had a job that doesn't wear me out physically or mentally, never had a Christmas where it doesn't end up being a competition with the family about who has the better life (which is not really a competition as that honour is always awarded to my ponsey-arse brother, who according to my parents has light constantly protruding from his rear end), never had a joyous moment where you need to pick up a camera just to record the memory forever.

Apart from when the cats were kittens and in their playful stage, don't think I'd had such genuine laughs in a long time.

So that's what being by yourself 24/7 does to ya, it gets into your head and you don't have a single thing to focus on.
But I am who I am so if I accept that then so should every other prick.
Anyway if all goes well I should arrive back to dump these pansies off this afternoon. Then I can go home, check on the cats and get back to my normal run.

**Elizabeth**

Well thanks to Larry feeding Kym's parrot wine and getting the poor feathered thing inebriated, we are now sitting at the animal doctors.

Rebecca is aware of this small diversion but is unaware of Larry's involvement in this latest hiccup; as far as she is concerned the parrot has the bird flu and thanks to my quick actions of reporting to her before she checks in with me she didn't see or hear Larry as he lay spread out across one of the dog beds in the vet's office snoring his head off next to a very nervous Fox Terrior.

Larry presence is going to hinder things again if I don't get a rein on him soon. And thank god Gypsy was awake enough to foresee the delay with Kym and alert Lizard man who was travelling with Cameron to turn off his phone so he didn't turn the truck around sooner.

It took all of earth's southern hemisphere nightfall to set that up. We couldn't come up with another reason for Cameron to come back to the shop as well, let's face it, Kym's shop is not exactly Walmart and Cameron doesn't exactly follow his gut, he thinks too much with his head.

Any more annoyance with his job and he might just quit to spite himself even though his gut tells him that would be a dumb move as he is where he is meant to be right now.

So Rebecca spent all of darkness time crunching numbers and the best solution she had come up with without interfering in any other soul's path was to return the flowers to the shop, easy done? Well no. Because Rebecca had to source flowers similar to the ones Kym sent to cater for the double-up of orders, alter someone's evening to get them there, which takes work because normally it's not just one person's time affected (you know those times when you had to get Sally to soccer practice and then you get a phone call to say you need to drop the work keys back to the office right away and Sally gets upset because she is going to be late and will miss out on being nominated for the state team etc), and if that wasn't work enough we had to modify the paperwork so it appeared there was a double order without getting anyone fired from their job as we couldn't find a single person involved that had a lesson coming up about vigilance so it justified the innocent mistake about the doubled order.

Then getting another soul to recognise the double-up in order to get Cameron back to the shop in time for Kym to come in and meet him.

Not to mention ensuring that the festival this year will break record profits to justify the loss of money they had to carry with the order of flowers and delivery fee. There is a little bit of upset amongst the festival council members at the moment but it's only a temporary upset, after tomorrow, they will see it differently and wonder why they were worried.

All those quotations like 'tomorrow is another day' etc, well that's us trying to tell you not to worry about a thing 'cos every little thing is going to be all right.

Actually I think Bossman had a song that he influenced one of his Jamaican clients to produce one time, it was quite a catchy one too.

We had it set up so Cameron was due to turn around and come back after he received the phone call that the order was not needed. Thank god Gypsy had foreseen a delay coming (not that she picked up on the fact it was Larry's influence) because thanks to Larry getting Kym's parrot drunk, we had to act fast and alter the plan so Cameron could get back here in the afternoon and not the morning like first planned.

So now we are just waiting for the parrot to be diagnosed with drunkenness and no liver damage.

The hairdo that Kym got yesterday is messy and does not look as nice as it did yesterday; but I guess she didn't have time to fix it. And the one brown shoe she has on her foot looks ridiculous with her summer dress, but I don't dare influence her to recognise this as I cannot afford for Cameron and Kym not to meet today. Especially now Larry is present; I must be on my guard at all times.

I haven't had a real good look at Cameron and what personality traits he possesses beyond the fact he is always complaining, never looks on the bright side of life, and swears a lot. But I guess it doesn't matter, Kym is smitten by this Nathanial at the moment, and I was so hoping Cameron and her would meet before her date so fireworks would happen and she would soon forget about Nathanial. If it wasn't for Larry and his little prank it would have happened, but now, I guess I am just going to have to trust that Cameron has what it takes to woo her away from Nathanial.

Yes you are probably thinking it's written in the stars and because it's a soul mate thing it will happen no matter what, but the truth is some people don't recognise what is in front of them and some drift off in another direction and never meet their true destiny.

We can only set the course of action, it's up to the true-of-heart souls to recognise this and act. We set Kym and Cameron up to produce a human being who is going to do something wonderful for mankind but that all rides on whether Kym or Cameron are willing to accept this.

The human ego is to blame. They tried it here in the spirit world but because we promote higher learning which requires high opinions of actions and behaviour, it wasn't going to work out.

Many use their brain as the link to their soul, which is not the brain's function; its function is to work the physical body. If you need advice on that one, talk to an animal.

And right now my senses are clouded; this is not a good sign as this means the outcome can swing either way.

**Kym**

I can be grateful for two things.

Harry has no liver damage from what they can tell. They seem to think he didn't consume a great deal of alcohol, just enough to send him into a sedated type state; and the second thing is the fact I was not reported to the RSPCA.

So basically there is nothing they can do, he just has to sleep it off. Mandy with her well-meaning attitude, was trying to make light of it once she found out he was okay but I am not seeing the funny side of it at all. It was so irresponsible of me. Clouded by my own temporary madness I could have killed him.

We are now back in the shop, Harry in tow, and I am trying to prepare the shop for the return order of orchids. I have to try and get them sold today, if I can't, it means an insurance claim and I'm not sure my policy covers returns like this, simply because I have never had an order such as this. This is another reason I am disappointed with being off my trolley for the past 24 hours, if I was here at my shop yesterday instead of gallivanting around buying dresses and getting my hair done, I would have thought about the insurance. I would have had things covered and I certainly would not have been sporting a sprained ankle and nursing a drunk parrot.

But then again I also wouldn't have met Nathanial.

I had thought about cancelling my date, after all it was the prospect of my date with Nathanial that influenced my negligence towards Harry. But I couldn't bear the thought of that at all, I like Nathanial; he is intelligent and interesting, not to mention handsome. And I guess like Mandy, he may see the funny side to Harry's inebriated state if I rung to inform him I couldn't meet for a coffee due to having a drunk parrot, but then again, being a bird lover, maybe he wouldn't see the funny side and I would never hear from him again.

So it may be a good thing to go on the date and not mention Harry.

After a brief conversation, Mandy agreed that cancelling the date with him may be a regrettable decision so she has offered to watch the shop again and keep an eye on Harry, which I am so grateful for. Tamara, my work experience girl is here again today but she is far too young to be here all the time on her own.

But this is not what I pictured my first date to be like. Because of the order coming back and time spent at the vets, I don't have time to rush out and buy another outfit. I could ask Mandy to duck home and grab something, I cannot run the risk of wearing my beige coloured knitted garments; Nathanial saw me at my best yesterday, imagine if on the second date he saw me, well, in my natural state.

I must really like him because I am starting to care what he thinks of my appearance.

Oh and now I'm in panic mode over a dress!

**Elizabeth**

Well, we made it to the shop without any further delays. The parrot is fine and so far Larry is checking out the shop without too much drama, if he can stay calm until Cameron gets here we may have a chance.

Things seemed relaxed here amongst us spirit people; Gypsy is having a nana nap in the corner with Kym's great grandmother. Lizard is with Cameron and Rebecca is in the back room of the shop engrossed in paperwork.

She really did take her earth life with her.


Tamara the work experience student has a guide with her but she is no trouble. She is a matronly figure, her hair in a tight bun at the back of her head, she represents discipline but she is here only to make sure Tamara is focused on the task at hand as she is easy distracted. They need her to change that habit because her destiny is to go into an important career in the aviation industry in a couple of years, so discipline and focus is important. Not sure what working in a flower shop has to do with flying, but each guide to their own.

Mandy's guide is nowhere to be seen which is not unusual, she could be looking over Mandy's children at the moment, sometimes we work with the inner subconscious. For example Mandy's kids are at school but of course she is always wondering how they are doing - is Bella eating her lunch? Is Elisa getting picked on? So to settle the mind and spirit we often check in on loved ones, then the main client is not so distracted and worried as they go about their day.

So everyone is quiet and going about their business except me. I am so wound up that I am starting to think Rebecca's energy is influencing mine as I am normally the relaxed one. Rebecca hasn't looked up from her task at hand yet and seen, or even sensed, Larry, but it's only moments away.

I have just decided she is going to have to deal with him, as any action I take only makes him worse. Like after I pleaded with him to behave last night and explained this mission is for a higher than high purpose, he goes and pours Kym's remaining wine into Harry's water dish while she was seeing Mandy out, and well, I wasn't there to see it as I followed Kym out to catch the conversation between her and Mandy, but I'm guessing it didn't get there on its own and Larry was looking guilty when I returned to him.

As a young spirit I haven't got to the stage where I can look back in the immediate past, that is a skill that only comes with age and wisdom so I couldn't confirm it was Larry but it doesn't take a genius to work out he did it.

I went out to the street to iport Lizard so I don't draw attention from Rebecca if things weren't going well. But he is reporting all is well and Cameron is on a smooth track to the shop by the time the two hands on a clock reach the top together.

I return into the shop to report this to Rebecca before she comes out from behind her screen, and see Larry sniffing around Tamara's guide trying to get a reaction from the disciplined woman. I walk past Harry, and Lizard's booming voice squawks in alarm.

Rebecca's head shoots up from her paperwork.

"What?!" I hiss, making a hasty retreat to the outside.

"The bird. It cannot be there," Lizard pleaded.

"Because…?"

"The male subject has a phobia of birds," Lizard panicked.

Oh yes I remember reading that in his profile, but that's just a childhood thing.

"It's in a cage," I scoffed, "he won't even know it's there."

"For the rest of his life on earth?" Lizard said in a dry tone.

"It's fine! Just don't tell Rebecca, we will deal with it okay."

Lizard looks nervous as I shut down my iport, almost catching Larry's beefy finger in the closing jaws as he attempts to poke the screen.

I didn't feel Larry's energy next to me while I was talking to Lizard, so I am only hoping he didn't hear the conversation; imagine what he would do with that bit of information.

It was bought to my attention that Cameron had a phobia of birds as I read it in his profile and if I remember correctly I was asked by Rebecca if I could look into Cameron's past to figure out what the phobia is about and see if it can be mended in case it impacts on his fate meeting with Kym. Well I didn't look into it for two reasons. One, I wasn't assigned to him, Lizard and Gypsy were; and two, it's a bird. It sits in a cage. Like he does, sitting in the cab of his delivery truck, if he doesn't like birds, it's because it is a reflection of him.

Anyway turns out the reason he is like that is because as a child he got attacked by a rooster.

No big deal really, if he doesn't get over it in this life he will probably have to fix it in his next life. So as far as I am concerned, falling in love with a bird lover is part of his healing process.

Anyway back to the task at hand.

So after diffusing Rebecca's concerns about Lizard's outburst when she called me into her 'office' like a naughty employee, and after I explained I hadn't briefed Lizard on our client's bird phobia issue so it was a case of miscommunication and then having Rebecca ask me 50 questions on how Cameron had overcome his phobia so it wouldn't jeopardise this mission and well, basically me answering those 50 questions with lies to cover up the fact Cameron is not healed from his phobia, all is quiet. And apart from Gypsy, who is still snoozing, everyone is clock-watching but for different reasons.

Tamara is busy emptying the window display in preparation for the incoming orchids. Poor girl, as fast as she is moving displays of flowers around, Larry is right behind her moving them back. In fact he is such a pain he almost got a reaction from her matronly guide. So I diverted Larry's attention by giving him some bubble wrap that was stuffed into a box Tamara had bought out to wrap up the garden ornaments from the window with and now he is happily sitting in a corner popping the air bubbles.

I'm only hoping it would hold him long enough for Kym to leave the shop so he doesn't follow her.

It's almost time for Kym to go and met her date; I can feel her anxiety building.

Or maybe it's mine because as soon as Kym walks out of here Rebecca's head will shoot up from her paperwork as fast as a rubber band snapping and she'll then use all means possible to stop her from going, including throwing me under a bus if that's what it takes.

Her reaction is going to stir Larry up as well. And as much as I would love this mission to be over with so I can get rid of Rebecca and earn my stars as a top spirit guide and have the chance of developing skills that would rock the kingdom for eternity, and even though destiny has been set in motion for Kym to meet Cameron for the sake of the future wellness of this planet, deep down I really feel Kym needs to have this date with Nathanial.

**Kym**

I keep hearing a very faint popping sound coming from inside the shop. Like the sound a bull frog would make on a still summer night. But as strange and annoying as it is I'm not concerning myself with that right now. I'm focused on my coffee date with Nathanial; I was even fantasizing about how it will all play out while I was on the phone to my insurance agent, who by the way, will look at my claim only if the order is damaged or lost in any way, so I guess this coffee date may have to be a short one as I do need to be here when this delivery truck arrives to check and document the boxes as I still have a tiny glimmer of hope that I can claim it. It's such a big outlay to lose. I also have to get those flowers into the shop display asap.

I have this burden piling on top of me today and I really don't care. Even hobbling on this ankle is not bothering me and I know it's my excitement about this meeting with Nathanial that is pulling my thoughts away from my responsibilities, and that is irresponsible of me as well; you only have to look at Harry recovering from a hangover to see proof of that.

Time has really passed at snail's pace this morning and the whole atmosphere this morning seems inaudible but at long last it's almost time to hobble off to my date.

Mandy offered to drive me but I think I might just take the bus; a final check of my hair in a shiny display vase reveals my hair is not at all sitting beautifully like the day before. Cannot blame me really for looking rather drab, I have had a bit of a shock this morning over Harry and didn't have time to fix my hair before I left. I don't have a mirror in my shop, never felt the need to have one, it's a bit vain to be checking your appearance all the time.

I know Tamara is looking at me sideways today especially in my new-look dress and my less than stylish new haircut; she is not used to seeing me this way. Previously my long straight brown hair would've been tied with a scrunchy at the nape of my neck and my clothes, well, a bit dull.

She has been coming to me for a couple of years now every school holidays, not sure why, as she is interested in flying helicopters which has nothing whatsoever to do with flowers, and she doesn't say a lot, just gets on with the task at hand. I know she carries a lot of hair product around with her and I should ask her if she would be so kind as to lend me some. Hobbling into my office area I called Mandy in and expressed my concern about my appearance, Mandy simply rolled her eyes in a playful way and pulled out what I can presume is an emergency hair brush and went to work tiding my hair.

Tamara, sporting a bit of a shocked expression when she approached the office, sheepishly grabbed her bag of tricks from behind the door and offered it to me.

Mandy suggested a bit of make-up and after a bit of protesting by me it turned out I had no choice but to sit there as the two girls set about making me over. There is so much screeching and laughter from all of us it certainly turned a quiet morning in the shop to a raucous one, even Harry has made a full recovery and is trying to make himself heard over the sound of female giggles.

Thank goodness we have no customers come in, I'm sure they would think they walked into a slumber party, in fact I'm having so much fun I'm starting to not think about my date.
Oh who am I kidding, this kind of female behaviour is always over a boy isn't it.
Anyway after several of minutes of being combed, drawn on and plucked by Mandy and Tamara, Mandy pulls out her rather large hand mirror to reveal someone I hardly recognise. My eyes look big and bold and stand out nicely, not like pinholes in my head; my complexion looks smooth and flawless and I never knew my lips could be so full and complimentary. Tamara stuck to my instructions and didn't put a lot of make-up on, it still looks like it's the natural me, only highlighting my features.

And my hair looks like it did when I stepped out of the salon. In fact the only thing letting my appearance down is my one brown loafer shoe and my hideous knitted winter sock covering my bandage, Tamera must have read my thoughts as she suggested taking the sock off and she will quickly paint my toenails with her super quick drying toenail polish so I can just hobble with one foot exposed.

Poor girl was not ready for my snappy reaction, she wasn't to blame, she didn't know my animosity for bare, exposed feet, I didn't know how to explain to her either as she quickly gathered up her products and moved away back to her other tasks. Mandy defused the tense moment by reminded me the bus will be stopping out the front any moment now, so I quickly grab my one leg aid and my purse and hobble towards the bus stop.

Strange, the atmosphere in the shop still feels chaotic although we women have calmed down.

**Elizabeth**

Things are not good, the place has gone wild.

And you couldn't shove it in Rebecca's face more than when Kym entered the office area with Mandy and Tamara, causing Rebecca's head to rise and turn slowly like Satan's Chucky Doll toward the raucous noise of the makeover happening in front of her, not to mention the reason behind it.

It was about then she came after me looking for answers.

And to make it worse Larry abandoned his bubble wrap when the laughter started, so as Rebecca was about to take a dive toward me in a statement of fury, she got tangled up in a dance with Larry. I caught a brief glimpse of her horrified face as Larry swung her around the room in a fast waltz, but it gave me enough of a diversion to hurry the bus up so I could get Kym onto it and away on her date.

Kym hobbled out from behind the screen chortling and smiling with Mandy, oblivious to the spiritual activity going on around her.

Larry slams into Tamara's matronly guide, knocking her to the floor and breaking his dance hold on Rebecca. Rebecca rebalanced herself and quickly proceeded to try and block Kym as she made her way towards the approaching bus.

I watched as Rebecca set in motion a white headed pigeon to collide with the oncoming bus. I can see how this will play out; the pigeon's collision with the bus would send him in the path of Kym, injuring his wing. Kym being the bird lover she is, would not be able to resist, she would wave the bus on and spend the rest of the morning nursing the bird, missing her date with Nathanial.

At this point you would think I should have just let it go, stand back and let Rebecca take control; but I cannot, I simply cannot, Kym needs this. And I need to find a way to make this happen without Rebecca thinking I am jeopardising this mission. She would have me sent back and banished as fast as Larry is getting a cane beating from Tamara's matronly guide for knocking her over.

Kym hobbled towards the approaching bus, I watch in slow motion as the bird approaches the oncoming bus, if I need to act to stop this from happening, it has to be now.

As I go to move to prevent the impact, Larry leaps in front of me, springing himself through the air; the pigeon takes fright from his presence and changes course. The bus rolls to a gentle halt as Larry hits the windscreen, spreading himself across the glass like a decoration.

Kym boards the bus with the help of Mandy and waves goodbye. As the bus rolled off with Larry still attached to the windshield, I cannot help but feel divine intervention is on my side.

And when I get back to headquarters I will find her and thank her.

**Cameron**

If I have any more fucking hold-ups today I am going to rip someone apart.

First it was some tosser towing a caravan who insisted on doing 40km an hour in a 100k zone; finally after the traffic behind me stretched back for miles, I got the opportunity to go around the useless twat of a driver only to hit Grandma and Great Aunty or whoever the fuck taking a Sunday stroll down the highway in their Nissan Micra! I swear to god they find their driver's license in a weetbix packet.

I don't feel tired and I keep reminded myself to chill out and just sit behind the slow moving vehicles, I'm not getting paid any more for rushing but for some strange reason I feel I have an appointment to attend and I don't know when or where this appointment is, hope this is not a side effect of being on this bloody road for too long.

I tell ya what though, I cannot wait to get back to the shop and unload these pansies and return this truck, I have never driven anything so gutless in my life.

And just as I was about to settle in and accept the fact I will be stuck behind Mrs Maud in her tea-cosy of a car, she exits off the highway leaving the road free and clear. Looks like I may have a quick trip after all.

**Elizabeth**

Rebecca has threatened me with more than banishment if I leave this spot.

She has gone after Larry and Kym in an attempt to bring Kym back, leaving me at the shop to wait as she puts things back on course. Even Gypsy has been told to stay put and keep her nose out of it. Mind you Gypsy was doing that anyway, Rebecca just made it official.

She wasn't mad at me because of what happened with Larry foiling her diversion, she couldn't be, she knows full well I had nothing to do with that. She is mad I allowed Nathanial to walk in and unbalance Kym's natural way of thinking. But now she has taken complete control of this mission, only pausing briefly to instruct Lizard to slow Cameron down a bit so she can fetch Kym and bring her back here.

So I guess for me this is it, I am under instruction not to partake in this mission any longer.

And I wonder what will happen to Larry for interfering. I am fighting every inch of Rebecca's intent with this mission. It doesn't seem right to me.

As important as this mission is, it hasn't allowed for the fact that Kym is a powerful and beautiful woman trapped in a time warp of self-discipline with her great granny's demeanour.

To have the only purpose in life being to marry a man and have his child, without experiencing the joy of feeling beautiful in her own right, to know there will be more than one soul in this world who thinks she is worthy of love and attention, is simply wrong.

The spiritual council is just another government, bound by laws and red tape. They do not concern themselves with personal growth unless it's for a higher purpose and for Kym the only purpose is to be a vessel for little Phoenix so he can go on to save this planet. For Kym I guess she will not foresee how important her role is until little Phoenix completes whatever it is he needs to accomplish. Unless she goes to one of our earth helpers like a clairvoyant or a spiritual medium, but I think they are blocked from any classified information so even if Kym did visit one of them, they couldn't reveal anything anyway which brings me back to Kym and the growth within herself she would never experience.

The important point of this mission is drawing closer as Lizard opens up the road ahead so it is clear now for Cameron.

Which also means Rebecca has fetched Kym and is guiding her closer to the shop.

The phone in the shop starts to ring; Mandy picks up and the nature of the conversation suggests to me the date is over and Kym is on her way back, leaving Mandy protesting at Kym making her wait until she returns to fill her in on her morning. As Mandy replaces the receiver sporting a grin of contentment for her friend, I know if I am going to do the right thing by Kym, I am going to have to go against the greatest power in this universe to save one soul from a life time of missed opportunities.

**Kym**

I am so relieved that went well.

I thought I was in for a massively awkward time when I first saw him standing next to the coffee cart as I hobbled towards him, his eyes diverted to my feet and it was only then I remembered I still had my one ugly brown loafer shoe on my good foot and an oversized grey woollen sock on the other, again I could kick myself for being so careless with my appearance. Although a positive is I feel so grown up with this make-up on, it's silly to feel grown up when you are 40 years old but I do, lovely and sophisticated.

The awkward moment soon melted away as I got closer and he greeted me with a kiss to the cheek. He had a faint smell of aftershave on him which reminded me of the day before when he helped me up from the payment after I took my tumble and the concerned look on his youthful features as he lifted me up and carried me towards the taxi. His smell and his charisma have me writing romance novels in my head.

He is just lovely.


We collected our lattés and found a park bench nestled under a shady tree and were soon engrossed in conversation. He has such a hero demeanour about him, like a noble knight in student clothing.

Time is a problem when you're having so much fun. As much as I enjoyed Nathanial's company and enjoyed hearing about him and his work, I had this annoying niggling urge to head back to the shop. Maybe because I knew the truck would be arriving with the returned order, and it just wouldn't leave me alone, like a monkey on my back I couldn't shake.

He must have sensed my urgency to return to work as he made reference to himself returning as well, although the tone in his voice suggested that like me, he did not want this date to end, and my feeling of nervousness returned about how to actually end this, do I suggest we do this again? Do I give him a kiss and tell him this was fun, was it that kind of date?

Nathanial suddenly looked awkward as well which made me all the more nervous until he requested my permission to ask a question. I thought maybe he wanted to ask me out again so I answered 'of course' with a faint excitement to my voice; imagine my horror when he sheepishly opened his laptop bag to reveal what appeared to be sanitary pads stuck all over the inside of the bag, even sticking out of the closed lid of the laptop.

At that point I had no idea what to say, until he started to laugh and jokingly accused me of making sure he didn't forget about me by littering his bag with my woman's products. I grinned back in a coy way but I had no idea what he was talking about or how he would think that.

Worse still I have no idea who put the pads in there, was he doing it to see if I would come clean and tell him he is crazy if he thought I would do such a thing, was this a test? But he seems impressed I would go to great lengths and said how he admires my crazy sense of humour, then he asked me on another date.

Despite the confusion, I said yes.

**Cameron**

I swear sometimes someone upstairs is playing silly buggers with me.

How come I have bloody idiot drivers in front of me for half of the bloody trip then all of a sudden nothing, not one car for the rest of the drive.

Not that I should complain as I am dying to get home now, I have had enough of the inside this poxy excuse for a truck. Cannot wait to get back to my bigger truck and back to my old run.

I pull up outside the small florist shop and put my hazard lights on. I rub my face to wake myself up and try to get some enthusiasm going, I'm debating whether I should grab a coffee from the asshole next door before I start. Or just get the job over and done with and get home. Sighing at my indecision I grab my paperwork from the dashboard, fill it out and go to step out of the truck. A gust of wind catches the door and almost pulls my fucking arm off, I watch the whirly wind as it winds up the street in a small twisting motion picking up a plastic bag and disturbing those in its path before promptly disappearing. Never seen that happen before in the city, open grain fields and flat land yes but not in a built up area.

Must be some truth to that global warming crap we're always hearing about.

I sit there for another minute; my whole body feels lethargic and I have to shake my head to keep my eyes open.
Deciding I'd better make a move before I splatter myself all over the pavement I step down from the truck with stiff legs and walk around to open the back doors. A woman on crutches comes hobbling out with a look of discontent on her face. I really cannot be bothered dealing with disgruntled customers, I'm only the delivery boy, it's not my problem her pansy's got sent back, it's between her and whoever the fuck ordered her product but that doesn't stop 'them' from taking it out on me, they all do it.

I jump in the back of the truck without looking at her or acknowledging that I noticed her coming towards me, in the hope she can sense I'm not in the mood to talk to people, and proceed to unhook my unloading trolley. Another reason why I hate this particular job is that I'm a truck driver, I drive a big truck, I pull up at my destination and a forklift comes out to greet me. This thing I'm driving is a poor excuse for a truck and if I have to unhook a push trolley to unload it, that doesn't make me a truck driver, it makes me a delivery boy.

I load the first 3 boxes onto the trolley as the woman appears at the back of the truck.

I force a polite 'how ya going?' as she starts on about how annoyed she is about having to receive her order back and blah, blah but I have to admit she did apologise to me for the inconvenience, that's a first for me.

Without responding to her apologies I asked her where she would like them, I have a suggestion where she could put her boxes but I suspect she is the type to put in a formal complaint if I suggested it so I have to bite my tongue and get this job over with. The pansy café owner next door pokes his head out the café door and throws a glance in my direction, his look of contempt toward me is enough to make by bad mood escalate. I pull my electronic delivery pad from my pocket, viciously tapping at the screen before thrusting it at the florist shop owner and instructing her to sign. Balancing on one leg aid she signs off and without another word I lower the tailgate.

A bloody awful screeching noise starts up and at first I thought it was the hydraulics on the tailgate; the woman also noticed the noise and in a slight panic hastily hobbled back inside her shop. I followed her lead slowly with my trolley full of boxes, a young girl held the door open for the pair of us, before latching the door to the wall to allow me to get the next batch of boxes.

As I placed the trolley flat to unload, my skin went cold upon recognising the screeching that had come from inside the shop. There it was; the ugliest feathered creature to roam this planet and what makes it worse, it's caged.

The woman with the crutches is trying to calm the stupid thing down so I presume it's her bird. How anyone can keep such a thing and actually call it a pet is beyond me, they must be sick. I head back out the shop for the next load and am starting to feel woozy; if the fucking thing just stopped screeching I think I would be okay but hearing it as well as seeing it is making my stomach turn and I am fighting the urge to throw up. Don't ask me what it is with caged birds that make me physically ill, I have had this hate towards them for as long as I can remember. Free birds are fine, I can handle them, but caged birds hurt every aspect of my body and hearing them builds a real deep down distaste inside me that makes me want to punch people.

Maybe I'm just a psychopath that hasn't had the balls to evolve. That was my private wee joke to myself, my way of preparing to take the next lot of boxes into the shop.

I'm in a bit of a cold sweat but I manage to take the next two loads without much drama, although the fucking thing is still screeching, the owner has moved away and is now completely ignoring it. The young girl spoke to me as I shifted the boxes off the trolley, but of course I couldn't hear her over the noise. So I shifted my ear closer to her.

"Someone must be excited to see you," she mused, referring to the screeching feathered thing who at this point was so loud you couldn't hear the traffic noise outside, I forced a smile back at the young girls' attempted joke but inside I was fuming, has this owner got no consideration for anyone? She's going about her business without a care that her bird is causing distress!
I stormed back outside to fetch another load, fighting my urge to say something as the bloody thing is now giving me a headache; if she didn't have it in that fucking cage it wouldn't be so loud.

Slamming the last box onto the trolley and thanking my lucky stars I only have one more load to go, I look up to the owner standing there; she was holding a bit of paper in her hand and opened her mouth to refer to the return document that was attached to the boxes.

149

She had the audacity to ask me if I could reload and deliver nine of these fucking boxes to an address downtown as a bit of a favour.

I couldn't hold it back much longer; the anger building inside me was too much.

"Look lady," I started, "who in their right mind would want to come here with that racket going on…" or words to that effect, I cannot remember exactly what I said, but it wouldn't have mattered 'cos her response was darn right rude either way.

And then it was on.

I have never met such a self-righteous stuck-up person in all my life; she accused me of being an animal hater and said the bird is just being a bird. So I told her how obscure her comment was about being an animal hater considering I'm not the one caging an animal to the point it's protests can be heard three blocks away.

That's when she informed me, quote, 'for my information Howie, or Happy, or whatever its name is, has had a traumatic morning and is just recovering', un-fucken-quote.

At that point I think I burst out laughing.

Another gust of wind appeared, catching the owners dress as she suddenly fought with one hand to keep it down; it caught up the dust and debris on the sidewalk and whipped them across my bare legs. The owner turned and made her way back into the shop, probably embarrassed that her dress made its way up around her ears, not that I was looking anyway, she's not my type so she better not flatter herself with the idea that I was.

The whirly wind suddenly disappeared again and I look up at the sky for any sign of unusual clouds but all seems normal up there. As I turn back my truck suddenly stalls and my hazard lights switch off. So I make my way around to the cab to turn it back on so I can get this tail gate up and complete this order. The bird noise seems to have stopped so she must have taken my advice and thrown a cloth over its fucken cage.

I start the engine again, put my hazards back on and turn off the windscreen wipers, weird.

Taking a deep breath and rubbing my face I'm feeling a bit calmer and thinking it may be a good idea to go and apologise for my outburst, not that I think I was entirely at fault.

The lady was out of line with some of her comments, but as a gesture of good will, I will tell her I will deliver those few boxes, even though I am hating myself for doing it.

Calmly made my way back to the shop and opened the door she had abruptly slammed shut after our little discussion on the pavement. I open my mouth to tell her the good news only to be greeted by three screaming woman ordering me to shut the door. Panic-stricken I do so and before I knew what was happening my body froze ridged as this feathered thing came flying towards me and landed on my head.

My stomach turned to instant mush and I could feel myself go light headed, I want to scream but my whole body is fixed to the spot, and nothing is coming from my mouth. A woman is approaching me but the ringing in my ears is so great I cannot hear what she is saying, all of a sudden the shock wears away and I start bellowing at them to get this fucking thing off me.
I can feel the bird fly off my head to escape from my fury but it's too late, my stomach cannot hold and my head is light. I crash to the floor, throwing the contents of lunch over her pale coloured rose display as I fall.

**Kym**

Back in the shop and after filling Mandy and a curious Tamara in on the details of my coffee date I am struggling to get back into work mode.

I told Amanda and Tamara about the sanitary pad situation and after much discussion and possible explanations including Mandy's 'men are from Mars' theory we agreed it may have been his subtle way of testing me and I should just 'go with the flow' as Mandy put it.

The phone rings and Mandy answers signalling the end of the discussion; trying to pull my thoughts together I glance outside in time to see the delivery truck pull up. There seems to be a weird feeling inside the shop all of a sudden, almost like panic and chaos, which is strange as Mandy is dealing with a potential buyer over the phone while fiddling with her hair and Tamara is moving a display aside to make room for the boxes about to come in.

Maybe it's me and my thoughts as I feel very unsettled so it's giving me the feeling like *every*thing is unsettled.

Tamara suddenly stops what she is doing alerting us with her sudden change in movement.

"Oh my goodness look," she exclaims, pointing to a small twister-like gust of wind making its way up the pavement picking up a plastic shopping bag I was meant to pick up from the shop's entrance earlier and moving rapidly in front of the parked truck before disappearing up the street.

Mandy directs her attention back to the customer down the line while Tamara and I glance at each other in bewilderment, offering each other a plausible explanation for the sudden and unusual gust which had disappeared as quickly as it had appeared. I hobbled toward the door to greet the delivery driver and apologise for putting him out with the return delivery.

Stepping outside, the weather seems perfectly still and calm. Very unusual when you consider what we just saw.

The driver looks busy and focused on the load in the back of the truck. Not wanting to scare him I clear my throat to let him know I am there. He greets me without looking at me and I proceed to tell him how annoyed I am about the order being sent back and apologise for inconveniencing him.

He turns to face me and asks where I would like the boxes. The look on his face tells me he would like to tell me to go and stick my boxes; in fact his whole demeanour is getting my back up. I did apologise for his inconvenience, which he has not even acknowledged.

His aggressive manner is enough to make me dislike him and I certainly will not be using his transport services again.

I sign the electronic device he rudely thrusted at me and hand it back to him. Roland, the owner of the café next door, gives me a wave as I head back indoors. Roland, or Rolly as he's known by his friends, often sticks his nose outside to see what's going on, he never misses a thing; mind you, according to Mandy he had one of his plant pots he displays outside his café broken the other day so it may explain why he is a bit nervous with the delivery truck parked so close on the cobbled pavement. Apparently he is still waiting for it to get replaced.

The sudden noise coming from inside my shop sends me into a slight panic as to what's happening, I hastily hobble towards the door and I realise it is Harry squawking at high pitch. Tamara opens the door for me and informs me Harry has suddenly gone mad.
I sigh at the fact, although I am relieved he is all good. He seems a little more hyped up than normal and his high pitched squawking seems louder than normal. I grab a piece of cheese from the counter and try to calm him down but it's hopeless, and he seems agitated so I think I will ignore him, he'll settle down soon.

Mandy finishes her phone conversation from the less noisy corner of the shop and informs me she has found a buyer for nine boxes of orchids if we can get them delivered within the hour. That would sell 900 of my 3000 orchids so I am really happy about that. The address is on the other side of town, not too far away; if Mandy was to take them, it would take her about three trips as her boot and back seat space may only hold three boxes.

Even though Mandy insists if it takes three trips it would be okay; I am thinking I will ask the driver if he can take them, if the company depot address is correct it'll be on his way, so I don't think I'd be putting him out too much, then it'll definitely be the last time I will use him for deliveries.

My goodness Harry seems to be getting louder, almost cannot hear myself think.

Reminding Mandy of what a gem she is for finding me this order, she jumps back on the phone to other buyers in the hope we can sell the remaining boxes. I print out the address and quickly hobble over to the delivery man who was loading another lot onto the trolley when he looks up at me with a pale face. He looks terribly distressed.

I was about to ask him if he was okay when he starts shouting at me. I was completely taken aback. I think it took a moment for the shock to wear off and when it did I couldn't believe my ears.

He was accusing Harry, a harmless little bird, of making him sick and he cannot imagine anyone would want to set foot anywhere near me or my shop with the amount of noise Harry is making and suggested ways I could shut Harry up. Normally I shy away from confrontation but this man doesn't frighten me at all, in fact he makes me so angry inside I want to explode; it's like years of anger just brewing, and all of a sudden it wants to erupt. I couldn't help myself, the words just spilled out like poison. I told him Harry has had a traumatic experience and he should show a little more respect for animals and stop suggestions of cruel antics. Then he accused me of being the cruel one for keeping a bird in a cage when they obviously have feathers for a reason, and that is to fly, before proceeding to laugh in my face.

I was absolutely fuming inside and had to leave before I smacked him with my leg aid, I held my dress down with one hand as another gust of wind whipped up sending debris whipping around my bare legs. If I wasn't fighting the wind and trying to maintain my dignity I would have made an angry dramatic exit.

And the only time Rolly from the café didn't poke his head out to see what was going on.

I stepped back inside the shop to tell Mandy to start packing the car when Tamara screamed at me to close the door.

Harry is flying around the shop, and in a panic I slam the door shut before he makes a beeline for it.

"Who let him out!" I exclaimed.

"We don't know," Mandy snapped, bewildered and stressed with Harry's escape, "one minute he is squawking at the top of his voice, the next he is flying around the shop!"

Well at least it's shut him up.


Sighing at the dilemma I contemplated catching him and decided just to let him settle down a bit first; maybe he just needs to spread his wings for a minute.

Leaving him to it, I informed Mandy we have to deliver the boxes after all as I have very little doubt the obnoxious truck driver will.

I have never had a man stir so much inside me and not in a good way; even Nathanial didn't awaken this much emotion inside me with his kindness. Mind you Nathanial is a sweetheart with a mild and gentle nature so it's understandable to be at peace and harmony in his company. This oaf of a man is not.


The chime of the bell on the shop door sends everyone into a blind panic as Harry makes his way in that direction.

The shop breaks into hysterics as Mandy, Tamara and myself shriek at the delivery man to shut the door. Confused, he does so, just before Harry can reach the open air of freedom. He circles, and lands on the truck driver's head.

Everybody breathes a sigh of relief, I really must get him back in his cage, this is not good.

A quick thinking Tamara locks the shop door before anyone else enters and Mandy goes to fetch a towel to corner Harry so we can coax him back in his cage and get this fiasco over with.

I don't know if it was Tamara locking the shop door or asking the truck driver to hold still but suddenly he starts swearing hysterically, startling Tamara. Poor Harry got such a fright, and flew off, which is just great as it is going to take us ages to coax him back now after the unnecessary racket from the driver. Not liking birds is one thing but acting like a two year old is another!

Rubbing my temples I feel a headache coming on from all this chaos, my thoughts drifted briefly back to my coffee date with Nathanial, the only nice moment I have had in this bad day.

You would think that the date with Nathanial happened on a completely different day to this one as it seems like a distant memory.

Mandy returns with a towel and a bird net, which under normal circumstances wouldn't be needed as domestic birds like Harry should be able to come to you, but considering I have a hysterical excuse for a man in my shop who will not calm down, a bird net seems to be the answer.

Actually, he has gone quiet?

Tamara lets out a small shriek as I spin around in time to see my roses covered in vomit and the driver faint in front of my eyes.

## 7

**Operation KymCam the first contact of the souls.**

### Elizabeth

There are two positives to this situation.

Okay, maybe only one positive.

At least they will remember their first meeting.

I cannot write just that, Rebecca will not accept it as enough of a report, but it's true.

We are each writing a report for Rebecca. She has asked us to do so while she is upstairs contemplating how she is going to approach the spirit connect when it was clearly outlined in this mission that this was our task, to put them in the same place at the same time. There was meant to be laughter and flirty moments and a sense of magic so it paves a course of action for little Phoenix to be born and save this planet from whatever it is destined for.

Instead there were harsh words, awkward moments and human expulsion of stomach contents.

I glance up as Gypsy and Lizard viciously scribble on their paper, well Lizard's writing is like a scribble, it's very difficult given his little arms.

There is only one explanation why things didn't go to plan today, Larry!

That's all I really need to write down.

It was Larry who premeditated the meeting between that Nobleman and Kym; it was Larry who prevented me from steering Kym away from Nathanial moments after their meeting; and it was Larry who interfered with Harry who ended up responsible for today's fiasco.

We had a chance when Kym came back from her date with Nobleman.

It was all very peaceful and all appeared to be on track with the universe's plans, until Lizard reported he had arrived with the subject.

That was enough to excite Rebecca, whose anxious energy stirred Larry, who at the time was happy in a corner popping bubble wrap. Gypsy, Rebecca and Larry sprang into action. That's when things turned chaotic, it was like a whirlwind of energies as Rebecca and Larry met at their anxious pace to get to Cameron and witness the first meeting; never mind Kym who was hobbling towards the door accompanied by Gypsy who figures she'd better do something to look like she is contributing to this mission. Larry seems interested in this mission as well, it's not like him to stick around this long, normally he makes trouble and leaves.

So as Rebecca and Larry's paths crossed in their haste to be present when Cameron gets out of his rig, the hostile energy Rebecca has for Larry escalates as Larry reacts to her with excitement and love. That's when you have to duck for cover. A bit like day clashing with night or waves crashing violently onto sand; it sends the vibration so high it stirs the still atmosphere conditions into a mass of molecules dancing together making a whirlwind stir and dance down the street whipping up debris in its path.

Lizard's scaly, bold presence diverted the whirlwind as it hit his scaly body and bounced past the front of the truck before disappearing. When the dust finally settled and I could finally get a grasp of what exactly was going on here, Larry was stuffed in a cage with Kym's recovering parrot and Kym was already standing at Cameron's truck trying to make small talk with him, which was not going well.

Cameron's defences are up and he has totally shut Kym down; but now I can see panic in Rebecca's eyes as she realises the initial spark of love energy hasn't ignited, she looks bewildered and confused. I know what she is thinking I can read her thoughts like a book; her bewilderment has lowered her charka fields and left her wide open.

The question is swimming around in her head, if this mission has been set in motion to reach its destiny then why hasn't the connection happened?

Our highest source, our Creator, sets our destiny. Everything is planned in perfect divine timing, every action and every moment is the piece to a bigger picture. I don't understand what has happened, the course of action set for Cameron and Kym has bypassed the critical moment our Creator set up for the pair.

Gypsy is sitting on the tailgate of the truck observing; our eyes meet in mutual confusion along with Rebecca's, as we observed the cold and callous energy radiating between them.

"I'm going to find out what's going on," said Rebecca, kicking into troubleshooting mode, "I have to consult with the Highest Council."
She exits the scene, skipping in front of Kym who is hobbling back toward the shop before disappearing. I don't know what to do next, this destiny was clear in my vision now I cannot see past this present scene, it's hazy and I cannot change the course of events to get this mission back on track, nor deep down in my heart do I want to, the whole scene is confusing.

Back in the shop it didn't get any better; all I could do is observe in wonderment as Kym's parrot hysterically reacts to the presence of Larry who is wedged into his enclosure and is fiddling with the latch on the cage that Kym has so firmly secured to avoid theft of her precious feathered friend. Kym, of course, cannot sense why Harry is in such distress and her attempts to calm him are in vain. Not sure if Larry was stuffed into the cage by Rebecca or he put himself there to get out of the way.

Cameron's defences are at an all-time high, a frenzy of flashing colours are dancing around his aura at the sight and sound of a distressed parrot as he goes about his physical task. Any moment now it's going to explode.

My iport buzzes on my hip and Rebecca's face appears on the screen.
"Find a way to get him to stay there for a bit longer," she instructs quickly, before fading out. My attention turned to Mandy who was finishing up her phone conversation from the quietest corner of the shop. The conversation was with a buyer who has brought some boxes of orchids that Cameron was unloading.

With a swift movement I danced towards Kym as she passed through me towards Mandy, I altered her thought process to involve Cameron in the redistribution of the flowers.

Cameron's energy aura is off the planet and between the colours of anger swirling around him and Larry's agitated attempt to free himself from his temporary prison, not to mention Harry's distress, the energy is reaching dangerous levels of anger and negativity and Lizard has ducked for cover underneath the flower sorting table.

Bang!

And there it goes.

An angry clash explodes between Cameron and Kym when she approaches him about the extra delivery; even from the bustle of the street outside the harsh words were ricocheting through the shop, cutting the air like icicles.

And then everything went silent.

Deafening silence settles and the vortex of angry energy swirling in the atmosphere comes down and bounces like a rain of colourful rubber balls. A gust of air passed near the side of my head as Larry spills out onto the street, the same gust causing an embarrassed Kym's skirt to blow up.

Harry dashed out of his cage and took refuge on top of the sorting shelf in the back corner of the shop. Then the energy rose again, this time into hysterics.

Kym entered the shop oblivious to her escaped feathered friend, the hysterical energy Mandy and Tamara are throwing out there is doing my head in as it rose to high pitch then dispersed again as Kym, suddenly aware the reason for the panic is Harry's planned escape route, slammed the door behind her trapping Harry once again.

Damn Larry; why does he have to be so chaotic. I was discreetly going about influencing Kym's growth by showing her what a confident lady she can be with new clothes and make-up, and Larry has taken it to the extreme but for now at least he has occupied the driver's seat of Cameron's truck and as long as Larry doesn't drive off down the street I may be able to salvage what is left of this 'important blip in time' that will end up in our banishment from the spirit world if we get it wrong.

There is talk about Mandy going to drop off the order and cut Cameron loose after he abused Kym in the street but no, no, no, no, that cannot happen, not now my spiritual existence is on the line.

I ordered Lizard to remove his cowardly arse from underneath the counter and get Cameron back in this shop before he drives off with Larry. Reluctantly he does so, as Gypsy nods off in the corner. Seriously that spirit needs to occupy a retirement village, or a morgue.

Kym is trying to get the bird back into the cage, but it is hopeless, so she gives up. A sudden change of energy again throws the shop into chaos yet again and the pitch drowns in my head. Grabbing at my head to quieten the noise, I zone into where the high energy is coming from and see Lizard gently coaxing Cameron through the shop door. Kym, Mandy and Tamara are throwing panic into the atmosphere and Cameron's aura is fading fast; a sign of fear as he slams the door behind him and Harry lands on his head.

Fear is an energy that has no substance, it's all an illusion, so Cameron's aura colour, all bright and vibrant, faded to grey then to black as he passes out on the floor, expelling the contents from his stomach as he fell.
So that is how the meeting of the 'two key souls destined to save this planet' happened.

Rebecca hasn't come back yet nor has she sent any instructions; the reports we have just written are only to keep us occupied, there is no way she will take these to the High Council. Those spirits are higher than the highest energy in the vast space of the universe. They can make anything happen; comets, asteroids tornados, volcanoes, right down to making the battery in your car die at that criterial moment you need to get the kids to school.

This mission seems to be low level playground cupid stuff and I don't understand why, if it is so important, it didn't just 'happen'. Rebecca knows damn well who has jeopardised this mission, the reports we have just written all point to one interference. I didn't want to do it but I cannot save Larry now. He sabotaged an important mission; the High Council has no tolerance to any spirit in their realm interfering in the destined path; unless it diverts unexpected obstacles put in the path by the devil and his disciples.

The devil, by the way, isn't all fire and evil, she was created to bring a balance of good and bad, as everything has to have balance. It's the bad physical people that have passed over into the spirit world she appoints that stir up the trouble.

And because there are no consequences for her spirits, things just go too far and pure evil can be created. So for every bad situation, we try and restore good and faith, but try telling that to a mother who has lost her child to a drunk driver or a widow whose husband had been sent to fight a pointless war involving religion.

But for Larry there is nothing I can do for him, Lizard and Gypsy have observed Larry's behaviour so I cannot cover for him. Larry will be banished.

There is nothing we can do except sit and observe until we receive instructions from Rebecca. And to make matters worse, just as Kym was about to call an ambulance on a passed out Cameron, Nathanial unexpectedly turns up at the shop along with his nobleman spirit and managed to get Harry back in his cage and help a very embarrassed and agitated Cameron to his feet, making Kym go all swoony and starry eyed for her young rescuer.

**Kym**

Well you can keep yesterday's fiasco, but wow what a day it turned out to be.

I slept well despite the excitement; it was a surprise I could settle at all.

Harry has gone back to his normal self but after yesterday I think it's best he stay at home. I think maybe the excitement was too much, he is sleepy today and I'm not surprised.

Nathanial showed up yesterday amidst the chaos with the biggest bunch of yellow and white roses. Ironic considering I just had my pale yellow roses tainted by the delivery driver who had fainted and vomited minutes before. And Nathanial didn't even appear at all put out that he brought flowers to a florist shop owner, Mandy may have had a giggle behind her hand about it but I thought the gesture was grand. He said he couldn't wait to see me for our next coffee date so he thought he would stop by the shop to see if I was free for dinner that evening. I was so ecstatic he took the time to drop by. Oh yeah and he also got the delivery driver onto his feet and managed to coax Harry back into his cage, so once again that man has rescued me.

Nathanial suggested to the delivery driver that he rest in my office for a while and even went into the café next door and brought him a cup of coffee. The delivery driver was more concerned where Harry was so to keep the situation calm, even though I feel the 'phobia' he said he has is a load of baloney, Mandy took Harry home. The delivery driver agreed to deliver the flowers to the buyer Mandy had arranged. I was going to mention the state of my roses he had managed to throw up on but I guess I am lucky he's not talking about suing me for loose livestock, so I let it go.

But my dinner date with Nathanial was wonderful, and I even managed to get another dress. This one was more designed to go out in the evening, it was a simple cut that seem to compliment a figure I was unaware I had. Even with my leg aids and one foot still in a cast I felt wonderful. I filled Nathanial in on the moment of madness in the shop earlier which he found very amusing.

But another day, another dull moment in my shop, I feel I have started to outgrow this place overnight. I feel like I could conquer the world and all of a sudden I have this overwhelming feeling deep inside of me that I am meant for bigger things, I just hadn't realised it till now.

And I guess I owe all of that to Nathanial. What a man he is, okay boyish in looks, but he is really interesting in a lot of ways. He does volunteer work in an animal shelter in the summer and feeds the homeless in the winter, he even takes his elderly neighbour to her doctor's appointments. There doesn't appear to be a bad bone in that man's body and he is interested in me.

I could talk about him all day but I have to tell you about the strangest thing that happened while out dress shopping yesterday.

After my dress purchase I needed to sit down and take the pressure off my good leg.

Mandy had rung the shop just as I was leaving to tell me she put Harry inside and she thought I was mad going out dress shopping on my own with my ankle the way it was but of course I was determined to look good, I merely dismissed her concerns, but I started to think she was right. Rubbing my good ankle whilst enjoying my coffee I had contemplated walking the two blocks back to the shop and calling Mandy to pick me up instead of jumping on the bus.

I feel uncomfortable getting into a taxi in my current state. You never know with having one foot so exposed and the reputation for taxis harbouring germs, especially on the floor with hundreds of other people's footwear passing through.

So just as I was starting to think that hobbling back to the shop and then getting ready for my 7pm date with Nathanial was probably biting off more than I could chew; the delivery driver appeared at the coffee shop. He must have been picking up a delivery as he had his device for signing the orders with him. Not wanting to face him again after the conflict we had earlier not to mention the throwing up over my flowers, I decided now would be a good time to go. I stood up to go but my energy levels were flagging and instead of a quick getaway it was a slow hobble accompanied by cramping in my good leg.

Jeepers, I must have had it in a difficult position when I was rubbing it, I fell into the first available chair but as you know the scraping sound of a chair is loud when you abruptly fall into it. I was hoping he wouldn't turn around and see me but he did. And the look on his face told me that now he has seen me, he feels obliged to say something to me. I wish he wouldn't; I wish he would just move on but in mutual contempt we both slap a polite smile on our faces.


"Do you need some help?" he asked retrieving my shopping bag from the pathway of oncoming customers.

"No, I'm fine, but thank you," I said back, willing him to leave.

"No worries," he said, placing my shopping bag gingerly beside my leg. My leg cramped again when I tried to move it away from the closeness of his hand as he placed my shopping bag beside it.

Sensing my pain I swear he sighed under his breath.

"Do you need help to get back to your car?" he asked in an impatient tone.

"No I don't have a car... but thanks."

"Bus stop perhaps?" he said.

"No, I'm only heading back to the shop," I said, wishing he'd just leave. I noticed he winced when I mentioned the shop.

"Okay then," he said, retrieving his cartons that were brought out by the café assistance. "Take care," he said, heading out the door.

I smiled a polite thank you smile as he goes but the dilemma that I had better start to move soon had quickly returned; the cramping was easing, so gathering my things I slowly rose from my seat again, grabbing my leg aids and wondering how the hell I was going to make it back to the shop.

There really was no reason for me to go back there, the place was all locked up for the day and the end of day till was done.

I spotted a phone booth down the road; I'll hobble down and call Mandy from there.

Picking up my sticks, a lovely lady held the door for me as I adjusted my bags on my forearm for the trip to the phone booth. Stepping outside I was taken aback when the delivery man was still there and standing right in front of me.

"Look," he said in a cranky but defeated voice, "I'm going past your shop, I am happy to drop you there, it's no problem given you seem to have a bit too much on your plate."

"Oh no, that's okay, really," I insisted again, "I'm having a change of plans anyway; I'm just going to phone my friend to come and get me."

He spots the phone booth across the busy road that my eyes must have flicked to when I said I'd phone my friend.

"Just jump in the truck," he says, like it's a delivery he is not wanting to deliver. "I'll take you home."

"But I live in Rosewood."

"That's fine; it's also on my way."

"It's fine, I don't want to delay you."

"Look, just get in," he said like his patience is getting thin and to be honest I was at the point where there is no way I was going to get out of this unless Nathanial came swooshing in on his white horse again. I reluctantly agreed and after a bit of an effort I am now sitting in the cab of the truck with my new dress for my date with Nathanial.

There is an underlying sense of awkwardness between us as he headed towards home. It's like both of us don't want to mention the several confrontations we had since he delivered my boxes back to the shop.

He finally cleared his throat to speak.

"Those boxes of flowers you redistributed made it safely to their destination."

"Oh, well thank you, much appreciated," I said turning my head his direction, now this is when the strange thing happened, because as I turned to address him, I noticed his feet.

He had nothing on his feet, no shoes, no socks, just bare feet out there resting on that truck floor. My stomach instantly curdled at the sight of his hairy toes. I focused my gaze out the window to keep my mind off it. I had always thought it was just my feet I couldn't stand to have exposed but the thought of his feet being exposed is breaking me into a cold sweat. I never had this problem with anyone else, even Mandy's children playing in mud with bare feet never bothered me, but the image of his is playing on my mind. It's repulsive but it's also making me angry.

It seemed like the longest journey and we didn't make much conversation. Finally we pulled up at my home and he seems cautious, like Harry is going to come flying at him any second.

"You right getting out?" he asked as I gathered up my belongings. I couldn't hold my tongue any longer, I had to say something as the bile rising in my throat is hard to contain.

"Why do you have no boots on?" I snapped, completely taking him by surprise.

"Why is that a problem?" he said, bewildered.

"Oh, just um…" I mumbled trying to contain my tongue, opening the truck door in my haste to get out of there before I throw the contents of *my* stomach up. My walking stick and handbag which was resting on the door crash to the curb below.

Shoot!

"I'll get them," he insisted, jumping from the cab.

I wished he wouldn't have, as my stomach is fragile. He seems to be in such a haste to get me out of there, and I am in just as much haste to leave too, but my problem is I have to take it slowly until I get out of his sight and my stomach settles down.

As he made his way around again my eyes automatically diverted to his feet. This stirred up anger in me like I have never experienced before and just as one foot made it safely from the truck to the curb below in his haste to get me out of there, my foot touched his bare foot.

That is when I lost it, my stomach all over his feet. He jumped out of the way from my shame, swearing as if I was doing this on purpose, once I was sure that I had stopped, I snapped and told him that if he had put his boots on this wouldn't have happened.

Of course this was met with hostility.

The yelling between us was so intense Mandy came rushing out with one of the children's baseball bats in one hand and the phone in the other, ready to call the police. The whole day's events, from Harry's escape, to my problem with his bare feet, blew up in a tennis match of exchanged angry words. It was a bit like a competition of who could hurt the other one with their own flaws. It was only when Mandy yelled '*enough*' that the dispute subsided and the delivery driver finished by telling me how crazy I was and that he would make sure no delivery driver in a three hundred km radius ever goes near me or my business.

I was about to retort by telling him I'll just send out a homing parrot when Mandy scolded me for my behaviour in front of her children, not to mention asking what the hell has gotten into me. This brought me back to reality as his truck roared off. What had got into me? Telling Mandy he made me angry because he simply wasn't wearing shoes seems crazy.

I humbly apologised to Mandy from the bottom of my heart. She explained how frightened she was, plus she was right, we do not know the man, he could be a lonely psycho cat man for all we know. Mandy softened after I showed her the dress I had brought for my date with Nathanial. Then I went inside to explain to her children that my behaviour was naughty and very, very wrong.

I reflected back on yesterday's events with shame as I went about with the daily routine of opening the shop the next day. Some people just bring out the worst in you and clearly that man did. I have had more conflict with him than any other person in my entire life, and I don't even know his name.

I feel like I have undergone a personality transplant overnight. Even Mandy snuck over to my place after I came back from my date with Nathanial last night to ask if everything was okay; she suggested maybe the change of life was coming or my biological clock was ticking; anything to justify why in just 48 hours I had gone from being somewhat reclusive and well, boring; to someone who dates younger men and argues with other random ones in the street.

I simply cannot explain anything more to her than Nathanial, it must be his influence. He kissed me last night when he dropped me off, not a long lingering one just a friendly kiss; it was nice though and we had such a nice time. We couldn't do anything like walk in the park afterwards, for obvious reasons, but he did make me promise that when my ankle heals we will go dancing.

I don't do dancing.

But I agreed to go.

I did quickly get over my obsessive disgust for that man's bare feet as soon as Nathanial arrived to collect me, but I have to admit I did glance at Nathanial's feet as soon as he arrived at the door.

I leaned on the counter of the shop thinking about my plight and it did become clear to me quickly that yes, as much as I admit my phobia for my feet being exposed has only really extended to myself, maybe I do have a phobia for bare feet other than my own. I wonder how I would react it Nathanial took his shoes and socks off.

This is paving the way for a whole new lot of fears. I feel my body getting fidgety and the very thought of it is intimacy on a whole new level. And Nathanial is so passive and quiet, maybe yesterday's rant over someone's exposed feet shows my true colours. I cannot see Nathanial thinking it was elegant behaviour, considering that was what he referred to me as last night when he picked me up, 'a stunning piece of elegance'. He is so noble; it wouldn't surprise me if he did have a white steed tucked away in a cupboard somewhere.

But even the memory of the compliment is not doing enough now to settle my anxiety down.

The shop seems very quiet today and the streets outside seem mellow.

Not that I am complaining. Lately it seems there is a lot going on in the shop, like there is people coming and going but according to the day's takings we haven't really been any busier, so I don't know what is going on, with my behaviour, nothing is surprising me at the moment.

A customer cleared her throat to get my attention and I welcomed her distraction. As I offered suggestions for a bouquet I noticed I hadn't even brought in the camellias from the cold room yet to be distributed to the local hotels for their daily display on 5 star floors.

After seeing my customer off I went to retrieve my key for the cold room to start packing up the flowers to be sent; Mandy normally does the deliveries locally and she should be here soon. I emptied the contents of my handbag on the counter to grab the key but it's not in my bag anywhere. I search a few more times before I call Mandy; I hope she hasn't left home yet.

Dialling her number it occurred to me the keys may have fallen out when my bag fell from that truck yesterday but then again I would have seen them surely.

Mandy is not picking up which means she shouldn't be too far away. The flower delivery time isn't set in concrete so if she doesn't have her set on her I can always send her home to get them. I now realise I've gone a whole ten minutes without thinking about Nathanial.
But the daily jobs are becoming more of a chore.

I busy myself with the task of setting up a display when I hear the shop bell ring again; putting on a pleasant face for the customer, I am greeted with the pleasant surprise of Nathanial once again, this time with a small box of chocolates.

Hmm, this attention is a bit much and I don't know what to make of it, is this normal? Mandy arrives in behind him and she greets him politely but I can sense her tone is frosty. I'm not sure why, maybe I have missed something, I'll have to catch up with her later to ask. He suggested we go for coffee and like a starry eyed school girl; I fling my bag over my arm and swoon off behind him.

**Cameron**

Never felt so fucking stupid in all my life. If it wasn't bad enough that fucking bird of hers caused me to have a serious panic attack and pass out right inside her shop door. I had her do-gooder boyfriend making a scene when I woke up, couldn't just slip away quietly like I wanted to. No, he made me put my head between my legs and all that crap. And he brought me a fucking latte, rather than normal coffee, and made me suffer through that before he 'deemed' me fit enough to drive my own fucking truck away, suggesting I see a doctor.

And while I was going through all that crap, someone had been in the cab and played with all the buttons. Luckily nothing was stolen. Darn kids I presume, lucky I didn't catch them; I'd kick their arses.

That would be the second panic attack involving birds. The first one was when I was a wee nipper and the fucking rooster attacked me badly yet again. Don't remember much about it but apparently I had to go see a head doctor and draw pictures to determine how crazy I was. That flower shop bird had me stirred up the moment I arrived there. Its owner didn't help much; her attitude made my blood boil. Some people just bring out the worst in you and she is one of those types.

But I have to count my lucky starts she didn't sue me for ruining her flowers when I chucked up my lunch. And as much as I didn't think much of her boyfriend trying to be a hero to impress everyone around him, I suppose I should be grateful he gave enough of a shit to make sure I hadn't had a heart attack.

And I offered to deliver her flowers, let's leave it at that.

So left there and reported to the depot about the extra delivery. Boss was pretty much in a good mood, apparently they had serviced my truck and I could swap back later today.

Thank god; I'm getting sick of this courier driver shit, I much prefer a heavy rig doing bigger deliveries. And after this morning's episode I'm also thinking I need to retrieve my balls back.

So after I made my last delivery, boss asked me to pick up some cupcakes for his daughter's birthday party, and have a cuppa on him. I think he realised that the run I had just done pushed my limits as far as tolerance went that's why he serviced my truck so fast I reckon, but all is good. I'm feeling a lot calmer now than this morning, I don't feel so wound up. And my cats seem to be fine according to the neighbour's kid so no rush, think I'll take it easy for the rest of the day.

But you wouldn't fucking believe it; soon as I start to settle down, I walk into the bloody pastry shop and there she was, the bloody bird lady again.

Didn't see her at first but then she sat in her chair that bloody hard the fucking think made a hell of a noise scraping across the floor. She saw me spotting her so I couldn't just pretend I didn't.

She must have been having a bit of a hard time with her ankle busted up 'cos her shopping bag was halfway across the floor and she looked like she was struggling a bit. Couldn't believe it, it's like I'm going to be paying for fucking up her flowers for the rest of my life according the fucking gods.

So I did the right thing and asked her if she needed help; she kept insisting she was okay when clearly she fucking wasn't, can't stand that. If you not fucking okay then fucking say so! Gave up in the end, nothing much I can do if she's going to be stubborn, that's her problem. I retrieve the two cartons of cupcakes, boss is running it through the business again I see, as the orders had to be signed for, he can be a dodgy bastard sometimes. Anyway, loaded these boxes in the poxy truck and went to leave; that's the day nearly done; I'm on the home stretch.

Then my fucking conscience decided to show up. Couldn't just leave, I had to make sure the crazy crippled bird lady is actually okay; she did look like she was in a bit of pain and obviously she is roaming the streets with only one leg working. Slamming the door shut I sighed at myself and headed back to the shop to tell her I'm giving her a ride whether she liked it or not. She was already making her way out when I insisted she take my offer of a lift.

Bit of an argument and to be honest I didn't have the time or patience for her bullshit so I basically demanded she get in my truck.

Anyway, if I wasn't being helpful enough for her, she hardly speaks two words to me the entire trip; not much of a conversationalist. Mind you, I have to admit I didn't want to bring up the events of the morning so I was trying hard to dodge the subject.

I ended up taking my boots off before we left; I kept catching a faint whiff of vomit on them and didn't want a reminder. About time my feet had a breather anyway, been in those boots for the past 24 hours. Arrived at her place and the most bizarre thing happened; she bit my head off for not having my boots on!

I was taken aback a bit and started to get paranoid that she was some sort of health and safety officer. In fact her comment got my back up so much I just wanted her out of there. I just hoped she has that bloody bird locked up; the thought of it being a few feet away again is making me nervous.

She dropped one of her sticks out on the curb when she opened the door so I ducked around to get it as it's taking her for fucking ever to get out; even with one bloody leg I'm sure she could go faster than that. Retrieving her stick I was about to pass it back to her; it was then she opened her mouth and chucked all over my feet.

I jumped back in shock. What the fuck! Where the fuck did that come from; was she bloody waiting for me to get round there so she can thank me by throwing up all over my fucking feet. And then if that wasn't sending me enough of a message she then tells me it's fucking my fault 'cos I took my boots off.

Well then it was on for young and old.

All sorts of things came up; she reckons that the bird phobia was in my head and I told her that's the pot calling the kettle black considering she just threw up 'cos a bloke didn't have his boots on. I'm serving abuse back at a woman who I have just driven home and I don't even know her fucking name. Yip great end to a fucked up day.

Then she started on other shit and I had no idea what she was on about, I think she's got personal issues and needed to yell at something; maybe that pretty boy kid of a boyfriend wasn't giving her what she needs or something. I need to walk away but it's hard to when I have so much to say but she's not giving the fucking opportunity because she won't stop with her grilling.

A woman, who I recognised from the shop, came out and looked like she was about to slap her; she had a phone in her hand so I'd better pray she didn't call the police; better get out of here in case she had, my log book for the past 24 hours isn't looking that flash. I drove away without looking back; sounded like the woman was copping an earful from her friend anyway; maybe it's her lover not her friend, looked like they were living together and there is a bunch of kids looking out the window. So maybe I'd better take it back; maybe pretty boy wasn't her boyfriend after all if this other woman is her lover.

Anyway what do I care, I told her there is no way I will be coming anywhere near her again.
Putting that behind me I went back to the depot, there is my rig, all gleaming and calling me back behind the wheel.

I started to gather my stuff out of this one to transfer, when I spotted a set of keys on the passenger side floor.

Fuck, bugger, goddammit! They have to be hers. Shit!
Which means I have to send them back. Well I don't have to… nah fuck it I won't, I'm sure she would have a spare set anyway. If she wants them she can come and get them, I'll leave them in the office.
Ah shit, can't do that. Then they'd know I had a passenger, they get a bit frowny about picking up passengers, so I guess I'm just going to have to send them back via snail mail.

## 8

### *Operation KymCam emergency meeting.*

### Elizabeth

I have been to more meetings since being assigned to this mission then I had ever attended in my entire existence, both physically and spiritually.

Anyway we have been given bad news.

Rebecca is here but first of all she had been given the news the same way we all did, by Bossman himself.

We got the news that there will be cutbacks in the spirit world; we are way too crowded and the amount of spiritual influence on earth is causing complications to the human race. Once you pass over, your spirit is there and carries on an existence, but there are now 180 billion living spirits, some have moved on to be reincarnated into plants and trees and of course new lives in different bodies but still, even the spirit animals up here are getting out of control.

Every spirit is trying to influence a physical human way of life one way or another; there must be a big shift in the universe coming if this is what is happening, because it has never happened before.

Anyway the hope for us four sitting inside Kym's shop once again is that if we succeed in this mission we will be granted clemency, I don't think the High Council realised it will be a dog-eats-dog world out there now with 180 billion spirits trying to keep their existence going. And with over 7 billion physical humans beings on the planet there is not enough to go around. This mission is only going to get tougher.

And no one really knows where you go to after a spirit actually dies; maybe you end up a speck of dust floating around in space. I'd take the banishment road any day; at least you still get to be around to watch what is going on.

Anyway after that news, Bossman took Rebecca aside to speak to her on her own. I have no idea where Larry went to, I'm only hoping he got bored and moved on, but after his performance yesterday, I would say Larry would have been the first one to go.

Gypsy doesn't seem to be too phased with this news; maybe Bossman should change it to, 'your performance on this mission will determine your future existence', then watch her sweat.
Lizard has been on this planet for the last 20 million years, I'd say he's had a good innings.

Mind you, he caused the big bang all those years ago when he crashed a space ship into earth, wiping out his own kind that had occupied this planet. That's when humans started to evolve, so indirectly, it's him that started all this.

We haven't been near Kym since the time before the nightfall. Apparently her great grandmother has awoken from her nap and is guiding her at the moment. And Cameron is on his own as far as we know, which means he won't know what was going on, he'd just be floating from one moment to another in this head.

We need to rethink this, I have no desire now to help Kym with her personal growth, not now that we have received this notice, but I have to say I am proud that she has taken her new found confidence, even if it is just a smidgen, and is growing it by herself. Well, unless her great grandmother steps in, then it may go backwards 200 paces. But maybe that was all that was needed, just a little push in the right direction. I think the young nobleman is the inspiration behind that growth mind you, which is great for her but not good for us, he really needs to leave the scene now.

"Totally agree with you Elizabeth," Rebecca said, returning from her meeting with Bossman, "the nobleman and his physical being need to go."

I must have my shield down if Rebecca can get into my thought processes; it's a hard one to maintain.

"So how do we do that?" snapped Gypsy, "that 19th century guide of his has some authority, he is a general isn't he; can't argue with a general, he is a high supreme, not to mention extremely handsome."

"That was 200 years ago Gypsy, his authority has well and truly expired," I sniffed.

"We just need to remove this Nathanial from the scene," said Rebecca, "should be easy enough to do."

"Yes well, now the spirit that is Larry is gone, all should be smooth sailing," said Gypsy.

As if Gypsy knew what was going on, she slept through 90 percent of it.

"What do you mean 'gone'?" asked Lizard nervously.

"You know," said Gypsy, making a throat cutting gesture at him.

I hung my head in shame for reporting Larry to Rebecca. Not nice to do that to one of your own. But I didn't have much of a choice; if I didn't do it, they would have found out anyway and that would have been much worse. I only wonder if he is floating around as a dust speck or worse, gone forever.

"Actually, he is not," said Rebecca.

"What?" I asked in confusion as Lizard and Gypsy said similar things in chorus.

"He isn't gone, he still exists," Rebecca sighed, "apparently he has been pardoned and is not to be touched."

Cries of outrage echo from Lizard and Gypsy as Rebecca rubs at her brow. I'm confused, why would Larry get a pardon when clearly he interfered in a mission that was deemed classified and important.

"So where is the line?" asked Lizard, "if one spirit can do that and get away with it, then what limitations do we have to avoid death?"

"I don't know where the line is," said Rebecca, "or why Larry's spirit isn't in the form of a dust ball; I'm only relaying my instructions from Bossman, which were clear. And that is to get Cameron and Kym together so nature can take over."

"But we did that already," said Gypsy, "it didn't work," she sniffed.

"I know that," sighed Rebecca, "but my instructions were that we still have time left, so by any means possible."

"Did you tell the High Council the meeting didn't end up like the normal destiny that was determined?" I asked in puzzlement.

"Yes."

"Did you tell them that Subject B would not even look at Subject A?" Lizard asked.

"Yes," sighed Rebecca.

"And?"

"And nothing, instructions were we still have enough days left make it happen."

"Well just remember Mercury is in retrograde," said Gypsy.

"Mercury is always in bloody retrograde," Rebecca mumbled.

I am stunned, Larry has obviously bargained his way out of this somehow and he must have moved on. Well with all those spirit guides floating around competing for their existence, I'd say Larry is having a field-day, so I doubt we will see him again. And as for the High Council leaving us out on a limb like that, it does mean they do have bigger fates to take care of.

Maybe we were just given this mission to keep us out of the way while they decide who stays and who goes, let's face it, it's not like Cameron and Kym are high priest and priestess material. I know their genes have been evolved to create little Phoenix so he can go forth and perform this magical thing he is meant to be doing, but why them? Couldn't they just combine the DNA of anyone to create the ultimate peace-making genius.

"So, plan?" said Rebecca, moving on from our speechless expressions. "This Nathanial has to go, how is this going to happen?" she asks, pretending she is at a physical world board meeting.

"Let me jot down some ideas," Gypsy said, turning a new page in her notebook.

Wow maybe the threat of her nonexistence *is* going to get her motivated.

"We could organise a robbery," Gypsy said.

"Yes agreed," Lizard said, "I think that would work well considering he has hero traits."

"Who, Cameron?" I asked, puzzled.

"No, this Nathanial," Gypsy said, scribbling down in her notebook.

"He has a war hero for a guide; this could work in our favour. And we can organise a masked man to do it, we will call it 'Plan Z', the z being for Zorro."

"I think Plan Z will work well," said Lizard.

Gypsy and Lizard have a vision on how the scenario will play out so I lean over to get in their line of telepathic vision to see what they see.

Oh my.

"No, definitely not," I said, "this is too much. I can see that leading to bad things, very bad things."

"Well, have you got any better ideas then?" said Gypsy, screwing up the paper.

Rebecca observed Lizard's telepathic vision.

"Agreed, Plan Z is a risk, get something else going, I don't care what, but for now let's get this pair in the same place. Lizard, go and find out where Cameron is at this present time. Elizabeth, where did Kym get to?"

I try to feel her energy around the shop but she is not here. She must have slipped out under my radar as we were getting the news; Mandy is here with her guide today, who seems to be watching us with interest.

I told her to mind her own business.

"Elizabeth?"

"Ah, one second," I said floating around the shop in search of Kym.

Rebecca's attention diverts to Gypsy to give her instructions and I have no idea where Kym went to, she is not in the shop. I could ask Mandy's guide where she went but, you know, I just told her to mind her own business

Lizard appears again in an excited state.

"He's on his way here. Subject B is on his way here," he exclaims.

"What?" said Rebecca, rising from her seated position as we gather round Lizard.

"Yes, he is on his way here, not in his truck, in a car with an object to give back to Subject A."

"Ohh a diamond ring," said Gypsy, "well that was easy, can we go home now?"

"That's great," said Rebecca, trying not to get overly excited and panic, "so where is Kym at this time?"

"Don't worry, I'm on it," I said, wondering where I should start to look.

"Too late, he's here," Rebecca said as the shop bells rings and Cameron enters the shop; we pause our activity and wait with bated breath.

Rebecca is giving me a look as if I had stashed Kym in a cupboard and she is willing me to hand her over.

I unscramble my foggy head and quickly zone into Kym's energy. Ah, found her! She is close, in fact just through the wall so I would say she is in the café.

So just gotta get Cameron to the cafe. He is not in work clothes so this must be a social visit.

Mandy spots Cameron and greets him with an expectation of an apology. Cameron apologies for his behaviour outside her home and we are instantly baffled by his statement, outside Mandy's home? He is apologising for his behaviour outside Mandy's home?

"Maybe we have been trying to hook him up with the wrong woman," Gypsy mutters to me.

Mandy smiles and said he is forgiven; he then asks if the owner is around, he didn't use Kym's name. Mandy tells him she is just next door at the café. He told Mandy he was just returning her keys as she must have left them in the truck.

Rebecca shoots me a look so fast and sharp I do a double take.

Kym was in Cameron's truck? Well this is good, but our mission isn't over so their fate hasn't been sealed yet.

And until this is sealed, any meeting between the pair is automatically beamed to us. So we would know if contact was made between the pair; we are authorised to know their every move. How did Kym end up in Cameron's truck? I mean who influenced that? It wasn't us, we were in a crisis meeting, and I doubt Kym's granny would let Kym go riding with strangers.

"If you want to know what happened, I could tell ya," said Mandy's guide, appearing behind me, looking at the four of us with slight amusement.

"You can?" said Rebecca.

"I was there," she shrugged, "the man who drives the big machine arrived at my client's home yesterday with the female who has the bent foot. She seemed to be repulsed by him and expelled the contents of her insides all over his legs and then well, they started throwing hostile information at each other. My client got scared at the behaviour and told them to stop and he left in the noisy machine."

As Mandy's guide relays the information, the whole scene is now playing out in my mind like a movie. Kym exits the truck and it appears Cameron has come to help her but she seems tense and then Cameron is startled by Kym as she has her head bent down.

Then there seems to be a whirlwind of negative energy as a haze of red angry light is darting between them; but how did she get into Cameron's truck, when did that happen?

Rebecca moves off, satisfied with what she saw, but something else in my vison has caught my eye.

There is another figure in that image. Mandy is there, along with her guide, Kym and her granny, and Cameron. But who is the other spirit that seems to be driving this whole argument. I can't get a visual; he seems to have blocked his aura. Cameron's guide gave up on him a while back so unless Cameron has picked up another one. But to my knowledge Cameron was left unguided yesterday.

"Did you see who this spirit was?" I asked Mandy's guide.

"Hmmm," she nodded, pulling a lolly pop from her month, "it was some hobo looking guy."

Larry.

"Boo!" Larry appeared through my vision screen like a 3d movie, scaring me. I should have seen that coming; wow my forward vision really needs an upgrade. Larry darted in front of me laughing as he goes and disappears through the wall to the café.

Cameron has indicated he is going to leave, placing the keys on the counter.

Rebecca's gaze slices through me again. And I can read her mind, here is an opportunity to connect this pair again and in a swift movement I arrive next door in the café.

Larry is sitting there beside Kym sipping tea with his little finger sticking out in an English tea drinking manner. The solider from the Napoleon era holds his hand out ordering me not to approach as I appeared.

"You have no authority to be here," he orders.

"That is my client," I said, pushing past him to get to Kym.

Time is limited and I need to get Kym out of here. The solider knows what I am trying to do and he is ordering me not to approach; and like a true military solider, he now has a musket pointing at my head.

"Kym," I yelled, trying to protrude my voice through the thin veil that separates our worlds. Kym rubs her ear, I am starting to get through, all she would be hearing at the moment is a low buzzing in her ear. I could just alter the thought process but I need to be close to do that and the Napoleon guy has me stuck to one spot.

Larry can see I am trying to get Kym to listen; he leans over and taps her arm before going back to sipping his tea. Kym rubs her arm and I roll my eyes. This is hopeless.

"Larry," I said, getting his attention.

"I need Kym back at the shop, can you help?"

"Not finished yet," he said, leaning over to see how much tea Kym has left in her cup. But then fate steps in and Kym glances up in time to see Cameron glancing through the café window before turning away and making his way towards his car parked in a tow away zone. Curious at his presence she excuses herself from Nathanial. But because she only has one good leg she doesn't move fast and Cameron is moving quickly, I cannot see how we can influence this to happen.

"Okay, finished now," Larry said, draining his tea and proceeds to push Kym from behind, making Kym hobble faster. Poor Kym, all she would be experiencing right now is a fast heart beat and a rushing need to catch someone.

Nobleman has released his hold over me and lowered his musket, it was Kym's free will to leave the scene and not my influence, therefore he cannot stop her, when this happens he must let me proceed to follow my client, at least he knows the rules of the spirit world.

I follow Kym outside as she calls out to Cameron, but of course not knowing his name she can only yell, 'oi, delivery driver', this of course is not getting his attention. I have a feeling he can feel she is behind him but is choosing to ignore her. What the hell is wrong with that man, bitterness is a real fatal trait to have.

Kym is oblivious to the fact he is ignoring her and continues to try and get his attention; just as she is about to give up I feel an energy pass through me in a rush, leaving me spinning.
Oh no, looks like the dreaded Plan Z has been activated.

Kym gets knocked to her feet as the mugger grabs at her purse which is securely hooked over her shoulder; realising he may not be able to get away quickly he pulls out a knife and quickly cuts the strap. Cameron, alerted to Kym's screams, reacts quickly to the mugger and scares him off as he gives Kym's purse a final tug and runs off down the street.
"We are at war," the Napoleon soldier declares, firing his musket into the air, "stop the enemy."
Nathanial runs past Kym in pursuit of the mugger followed by his noble guide.
Cameron rushes over to Kym's side.

"See, told ya it would work," Gypsy said, munching on a bag of popcorn while I retrieve my beating heart after it leapt from my chest in fear of Kym getting in harm's way... well I don't have a beating heart, but if I was a physically being, I would have died from a heart attack by now.

"It could have been much worse," I snapped.

"Oh rubbish," Gyspy scoffed, "look, he's getting down on one knee."

"That's because she is hurt," I retorted.

Kym's bad foot is bleeding through her sock and Cameron is trying to remove it. Kym is fighting him all the way, insisting he doesn't take her sock off. Cameron is trying to help but there is great panic in her eyes. There is a small crowd of onlookers gathering and with their guides in tow it's very crowded out here.

Mandy has arrived and Kym asks her to take her to the hospital. Cameron offers to take Kym but Kym is insisting she doesn't want to put him out. And Mandy is also suggesting that Cameron can take her while she waits and deals with the police, there seems to be a lot of fight and resistance going on, and Cameron is still trying to tug at the sock making Kym more agitated.

Mandy left the scene to call the police and then I saw it. It was like time stood still for a moment, Cameron and Kym locked gazes and a high zap of energy past between them. I thought this was it, I thought this must be the moment that seals their fate but as quickly as the energy rose it disappeared and time sped up again.

Oh, because Nathanial has returned, along with Larry and the noble guide. He has her purse and Kym is looking all ecstatic and happy, Nathanial waves a taxi down and thanks Cameron for his goodwill but insists he will take Kym to get seen to.

Cameron doesn't seem to argue; he just gets up and leaves without another word to Kym. Kym seems to be so wrapped up in Nathanial's heroism she hasn't even noticed Cameron has left.

I watch as Nathanial carries Kym to the waiting taxi, followed by his guide and Larry.

Hmmm, I think I need to have a little chat with Larry.

"Oh well," said Gypsy, throwing her popcorn bag over her shoulder, "back to the drawing board."

**Kym**

Well it's been just over a week of ordered rest and I can finally go back to work.

It's funny because just a week ago I felt I had outgrown my little shop, now I cannot wait to be back there.

Mandy and Tamara have been fantastic, Tamara has gone back to school but after my mugging she did some hours after school to relieve Mandy and showed me how responsible she is to lock up.

And of course Nathanial has been great, he has been around every day feeding my birds and making sure I am okay.

He got his picture in the paper with a story about retrieving my purse from the mugger and running him down; very brave of him considering the mugger was twice as big as him. Apparently Nathanial managed to grab him when he attempted to run around the side of a pole which knocked him sideways; he then staggered to control his balance, allowing Nathanial to catch up and grab him before he corrected himself and ran off.

Something like that anyway, the story seems to change slightly every time he tells it; I guess it must have been quite the experience for him, putting his own safety at risk to retrieve my dignity.

I can imagine he wouldn't really remember exactly how it all unfolded, but the good news is all is well, my already sprained ankle suffered a few cuts and grazes and swelled up to the size of a pumpkin but after a week resting at home on painkillers I can walk normally again.

At the hospital they took my sock off to reveal I was bleeding; not badly but my thoughts drifted back to something the delivery driver said to me. His words hit me like a lead balloon and I cannot shake it.

Nathanial has been very sweet, he even spied my old dull clothes in the wardrobe while he was looking for another robe and at first I thought he was going to run a mile, but sensing my embarrassment he has been joking with me all week about holding onto clothes in the hope they will come back into fashion, he doesn't seem at all phased that I wear knitted skirts and knee high stockings.

Despite all that, he seems to like me, a lot; and I'm guessing we are now in a relationship, although it's never been officially mentioned. By the fourth day of him being here, I thought I should take the biggest step and ask if he wanted to sleep over.
Mandy was great in giving me advice, even though she voiced her concern that she feels he has been suffocating me since we met.

The asking if he should sleep over was actually her idea, even though I agreed whole heartedly with her, she gently tried to warn me that if we do end up in bed, be prepared for him to back off, so I took the risk, very unlike me.

But it wasn't like that at all, in fact I was more embarrassed when he took my hand and said as much as he wanted to, he was saving himself for marriage. So he did spend the night, but on my sofa.

He seems to have old fashioned values and seems to thrive on coming to my rescue and I think that is why he likes me, which is fantastic but something doesn't feel right. But I suppose I'm not used to all that attention. I'm putting my doubts down to fear of the unknown.

But getting dressed, I look down at my feet and think about that day I was mugged. That delivery driver knew why I reacted the way I did. He is the only person so far in this entire galaxy that understood why I won't allow my bare feet to touch exposed outdoor elements. And when he said it aloud, it was like time stood still. I cannot recall if I asked him how he knew that, it all happened too fast.

But anyway I shouldn't dwell on that, I have to get to the shop for the start of my brand new life on two functioning legs.

I am super excited; tonight Nathanial is taking me to a Charity Ball, it's just one of the many charities he supports, studying human rights I guess he has to show some interest in a charity . It's meant to be very fancy, $150 a head apparently. I have nothing to wear as per usual so he is meeting me for lunch and we are going to go and hire a gown. I throw my stockings on and slip into my shoes. I still have the sandals I wore the day I hurt my ankle but they seem like a bad omen now so I should get new ones.

The doctor told me that probably the reason my foot slipped in them was because of the nylon stockings. Strappy sandals are designed to be worn without socks of any kind, but I couldn't exactly tell him that if my bare feet touched the ground it will leave a DNA imprint that can be traced and then tracked, and that won't be good when I need to protect my future child from dark forces that will want to cease him for his knowledge when I try and hide him in a cave!

Okay I finally said it out loud. It is a dream I have been having repeatedly ever since I can remember. Sometimes the feelings are so strong I think it was real. Mandy has brought to my attention in the past that both my mother and aunty had been known to take medication for a chemical imbalance in the brain, so it could be that I could just have a mental illness of some type.

Not that I am off the rails; I just have strange little phobias and I have my reasons for having them, it doesn't make me crazy. I have never been to the doctor to discuss this; it has just been my little secret.

Until the delivery driver tried to take my sock off when I got mugged. I fought with him with panic rising at the thought of my foot being exposed and making contact with the pavement.
That's when he realised the reason for my panic; carrying it around in your head is one thing but when someone says it out loud it changes things.

Right, I must snap out of this and get to work.

**Elizabeth**

We are running out of time and options.

Rebecca is ready to kill; Lizard cannot get Cameron anywhere near Kym for the past week and a bit while that stupid medical person insisted she rest at home. The dynamics changed because even if we could get Cameron anywhere near Kym, Nathanial is there. Guarding her like a queen.

Nathanial is heavily influenced by that guide of his; in a panic, Rebecca went to go and see Bossman to see if there was some injunction we could get to remove the solider guide so we could at least steer Kym in the right direction, but Bossman said the guide is not interfering with the mission directly, he is merely doing his duty as a guide. And it's an entirely different matter.

And all we seem to do is have meetings, but even with our influence in altering the course of action, there is nothing that we have come up with that will inflame Cameron's free will to come anywhere near Kym.

Lizard has been guiding Cameron and I have a feeling that this is where Lizard will continue to spend his days if we get through this without being turned to dust.

So one earth day is just moulding into another. And time is ticking.

But it hasn't been all a waste of time, because I have been observing Larry. He hasn't left Kym's side since he turned up in the street that day and he seems to be encouraging the behaviour between Nathanial and Kym.

But at the same time he seems to be playing both sides.

He is hard to track down, keep still or talk too. Larry is a spirit who has two sides to himself. When he was a physical being, he was a simple man, crippled mentally by an accident involving a horse. Before that he was normal. When he passed over he carried the two personalities over, the Larry before the accident and Larry after the accident. He chooses the later, but I have a very strong feeling all of this is just a strategy. Like a game of chess; but he seems to be playing against us for the same result.

I am convinced Larry knows more about this mission then what we have been told.

I have come to a quiet place in the universe to ponder this situation. There is a jigsaw of a bigger picture floating around here and I need to put the pieces together to see it.

Rebecca will not be happy with what I am about to suggest but time is ticking and I can feel the universe reacting to the coming change.

I know why we have been given the time we have been given, not because Kym's fertile eggs will shrivel up and disappear, but because the planets are shifting and they are almost in line and this is going to affect everything on earth. Some humans are already feeling the change, some may get migraines, others are feeling depressed and some simply cannot get out of their own way. We now have over 180 billion spirits roaming around on this planet and the world seems to be in chaos at the moment, the greedy are pushing poverty to those less fortunate, the religions of the world are feeling intense with the universal changes so the terrorism and killings are happening, and mother nature has just had a gutsful of the behaviour so she is spilling up everything from tornados to earthquakes.

And us spirits are running round trying to right the wrongs, to save us from disappearing from the universe forever.

Why does this mean Cameron and Kym have to get together before the plants align? It is because everything is set in perfect divine timing? If Phoenix is conceived any later then intended then the course of time will be altered? And we will all disappear?

So why send us, four amateur guides, to deal with a mission so important that it could impact humanity, and life as we know it will cease?

Because there are important things that Cameron and Kym need to acknowledge first. Knowledge and acceptance of things that will enable them to manage things in the future. Of course. That is our job, we are spiritual guides, we are the ones that teach humans lessons on earth during their life span so they don't carry them over to the new world.

Now I just have to convince Rebecca that the path we need to go down is one that is necessary to change this mission. But first, I need to consult with Larry.

## 9

### Kym

I have to turn the news off. I am saddened with the amount of bad news on it lately, natural disasters, killings, planes going down; the world has gone mad.

I have just returned home from getting my hair put up and it looks lovely, twisted into an elegant bun at the nape of my neck. Nathanial and I had a great afternoon picking out a gown for this evening; he even teased me about buying a brown checked kilt to match my brown loafers but we managed to choose a stunning and elegant red gown that matched his tie.

And closed-in toe shoes, so I can wear my stockings thank goodness. I got around that one with Nathanial by telling him heels and open toed shoes may not be good for my ankle.

He is also telling anyone who is listening about how he ran down my mugger and got my purse back; I know it was a brave thing for him to do but the story is really starting to wear thin.

Mandy and the girls have come over to help me get ready for the occasion; Mandy is so impressed with my hair she cannot help but look at me like I am some type of alien. Nathanial doesn't drive so he has ordered us a taxi in two hours and has gone home to get changed before coming back to collect me. Mandy has finished putting the finishing touches on my make-up while the girls painted my nails.

Then after the final touches to my personal self were done, it was time I wriggled into my ball gown.

As the satin fell over my body I suddenly felt like Cinderella, and after slipping my stocking covered feet into my flat closed-in shoes, I came out of my bedroom to my waiting support party.

Mandy was stunned and for a fleeting moment I thought she was about to say I look ridiculous but in fact she said the opposite with a tear in her eye. We poured a glass of wine and sat and chatted. Mandy is getting all sentimental at the changes in me over the last couple of weeks and wanted to know why the sudden change in attitude to life.

I laughed at her innocent approach and told her it all started with her encouraging me to think about getting my hair done by leaving her hairdresser's card discreetly on my bathroom counter. She looked puzzled and said she didn't leave a card as she doesn't have any cards; her hairdresser's number is stored in her mobile.

We decided it must have been one of the kids and then joked that my hair must have been bad if the kids felt they had to intervene. Mandy even made reference to the fact that I am now buying wine, and drinking it and not storing unwanted bottles away for a rainy day. We scoffed and joked about the antics of the past couple of weeks; there's been more drama packed into these two weeks then I have had my entire life.

Mandy started having me on about the fact I couldn't drive a new pair of shoes.

And I brought up about the delivery driver and how Harry tormented him after he recovered from his hangover.

"Oh, he came in this afternoon," said Mandy, finishing a sip of her wine, "the delivery man. He had to drop off a glazed pot to the café next door or something; he was just asking how you fared after your attack."

I didn't know what to say, I was instantly taken aback by Mandy's statement and was about to ask her what she told him when the kids ran over to the door.

"Nathanial's here," they cried, excited to see the look on his face when I open the door.

Kids are funny, it's the little things.

We arrived at the ball and it wasn't a grand, grand affair but still very nice. It was held in the conference room of a hotel; the foyer and staircase looked the part as we walked together with our arms linked. Nathanial looks smart in his suit and he told me I look beautiful, well what else was he going to say, really, I looked average. Half of his university buddies were here and I feel like a granny compared to them and the way they talk.

Nathanial is treating me like a trophy the way he is showing me off to his friends. They seem impressed he is dating an older woman, not that they have given any verbal indication this is the case but their underlining tone suggests they are high fiving Nathanial for bagging the older woman.

Or maybe I am just being sensitive, after all most of his uni pals have dates the same age as them and all of them have bodies on them like models and skin so youthful I feel like I should be reading them bedtime stories, not conversing with them over a cocktail.

He's relaying the hero story again, it's getting old and clearly some of his buddies have heard this story before as they seem a bit tired of it as well. The naughty streak I had when I first met Nathanial has crept back in and I have the urge to borrow the hostesses pen over there, rip a piece of the charity poster off, construct a hero medal from it and pin it to his perfectly pressed dinner jacket.

There is something about Nathanial that is bugging me tonight. But he is one of the very few boyfriends I have ever had, so I really think I need to snap out of this mood, it's not like I have them lining up at the door.

His suggestion of a drink has saved the moment and I do need another wine;

I giggled at myself as two weeks ago there was no way I would go out after 7pm and there is certainly no way I would be sipping wine in a ball gown.

Because he is studying human rights he attends a lot of charity balls for the different organisations. This one is organised for the recent natural disasters that have been happening, it's going to support the kids. I feel inspired by all the different stories of hope that are plastered on posters all over the wall. I also feel like a first world hypocrite with this dress on pretending I know exactly what they are going through, I feel it's just a showcase of glitz and glamour to say 'hey we care', but really if that was the case some of the people here who can clearly afford it, would get on a plane and go to these countries and roll up their sleeves and rebuild communities, but they'd rather sip champagne and talk about it.
Nathanial asks if I am okay and I assure him I am, it's about time I snap out of my judgmental mood and enjoy the evening.

Dinner is served and I try to engage in conversation with people I do not know but all along my mind is on the dance floor, I cannot dance and I have not mentioned this to Nathanial. Maybe I could milk the sore ankle for a bit longer but given I have walked around most of the afternoon perfectly fine, I cannot see that working out.

The more anxiety I feel about the dancing, the more I feel the urge to start a food fight, especially at the young woman sitting opposite me, who is all of 21 years of age and acting like she has cured cancer.

I have no idea what has gotten into me tonight, I feel like I have two personalities fighting for the right to take centre stage. I drown the urge in alcohol through most of the dinner talk, watching Nathanial as he engages in conversation with another young lady, I can just make out what he is saying and it's clear he's telling the mugging story again. I take another gulp of my champagne, I feel like a fish out of water amongst these people, who as nice as they are, seem not to care about bigger issues.

The plates have been cleared away and the music has started. Nathanial has indicated to me to dance, so I saw this as my opportunity to slip away to the bathroom in the hope that he would ask another lady to dance while I'm gone.

It wasn't till I got to the bathroom I realised I'm a little tipsy. I don't like being in this state, not being in total control of my body. And I am getting the strangest urge to take the full roll of toilet paper that is staring me in the face and decorate the toilets with it. I think it's best I excuse myself and get a taxi home before I stuff cream cakes in Nathanial's ears.

I walk back out to the function and the music is playing with my senses, I have never really danced before but my feet have the urge to move, everyone is in a well-coordinated dance of what I believe they call the Gypsy Tap, but not me.

I am now dancing my own dance as the music takes hold; the excitement seems to surge through me as I twist and turn though the couples on the dance floor. The more I dance, the faster and more confident I feel; I don't care everyone is watching me or that some are getting cranky with me as I hitch my skirt up from around my ankles and kick my heels up. Nathanial is trying to catch me and I find it hilarious the way he is politely trying to get my attention as I lead him on a dancing chase around the circle of couples. He doesn't look comfortable with me and to be honest I really don't care. I move into the middle and spin around. I keep spinning and spinning until I hit the floor.

I lie there in a fit of laughter as Nathanial comes rushing over. He asks if I'm okay and I tell him I have never felt better. He then helps me up and suggests we go out for some fresh air. His friends are all cheering me on for crashing the dance floor as I am led out by him, and I think that is why he's feeling a bit put out. It's because he is not the hero in the crowd for once.

I was certain Nathanial was taking me out for some air to tell me he doesn't want to see me anymore. A small part was dreading it but another part was kind of willing it to happen. But no, it appears I had misread him. He wasn't uncomfortable with me at all; he was more concerned I was going to do more damage to my ankle. And the urge to play games and cause trouble had disappeared. I'm starting to think I have multiple personalities, I know I am going to be horrified with myself in the morning for dancing in public while slightly intoxicated. This is unlike me at all.

We sat down in front of this beautiful fountain in the foyer of the hotel and talked. It seemed like we talked for an eternity, well to be honest, and this is something I have been noticing lately, it's Nathanial that does most of the talking; mainly about all the good deeds he has done. He is always talking about that, even at our coffee dates, but he also told me he loves the spontaneous, crazy things I do and he seems very accepting and smitten by me. I told him not to expect it too much as I don't do a lot of spontaneous things, he scoffed a bit at this like I was joking.

And then somehow we talked about life. It was then I realised I wanted a baby. I mean I could have a baby, I'm not past having one, and then somehow, somehow, well, Nathanial asked if I would be interested in getting married to him, and well, I said yes.

**Elizabeth**

I finally tracked down Larry; it wasn't hard to do but he has been dodging me this past earth week.

Of course he had to follow Kym to the ball, he couldn't help himself. I watch him for a while as he attempted to rip a poster off the wall, throw food at the table opposite Kym and then succeeded in dancing her round the dance floor, spinning her around so fast she fell over.

Nathanial once again came to her rescue and they walked off into the foyer. That's when I thought it was about time Larry and I talked. He protested at first saying he 'doesn't like me', as if that was going to deter me. But after dragging him by his ankles around the floor and sitting on him while he kicked and screamed like a toddler, he finally decided to talk because I promised him he can throw food at the woman who is here for her own greedy agenda. Honestly that woman's guide needs to be removed, she's hardly curing cancer!

Larry confirmed what I had suspected and that he was put into this mission to throw a spanner in the works by Bossman.

I wasn't surprised; I know the purpose behind it now. Very risky on the High Council's part but I guess it comes down to what we have always follow. Love, faith and trust.

But just as we thought we had it figured out and Larry and I were working out the finer details of the final plan for this mission, left unguided, Kym agreed to marry Nathanial.

So the urgency is much greater now that Kym's intuition is blocked by the thought of marrying Nathanial. The earth is getting angry and we don't have much time.

*10*

**Cameron**

What a fucking week.

I'm back in my normal truck, which is great, but the boss has been hammering me with long distance pick-ups, and I haven't been feeling too shit-hot, thought I was coming down with some type of flu, probably a bird flu from that mangy bird that landed on my head in the flower shop.

But it never came to anything so I just put it down to stress again. I reckon the reason I have been feeling a bit out of sorts was because of a weird thing that happened last week, can't make head or tail of it. Anyway speaking of that, I dropped by earlier to see that woman who owns the florist shop, you know the one who I have the urge to fight with every time I see her. Yeah well last week after I had given her ungrateful arse a ride home in my truck only to have her thank me by throwing up all over my bare feet, she left a set of keys there, I was going to post them back but I grabbed a fucking heart and decided to drop them back off.

Anyway I had a day off; after the boss decided my logbook was too dodgy and stood me down for 24 hours, so I rock up there to drop the keys off. She wasn't there but her friend was, the one she lives with. Anyway the friend expected an apology from me and fair enough, I did frighten her a bit.

So after I explained that I was a bit taken aback with her friend, whose name I understood is Kath or something, being sick all over my feet, she forgave me and said her friend was next door at the café.

I decided to let it go and just move on, so I handed the keys over and decided to get on with my day. Anyway without rambling on too much, I got outside and that fucking conscience took over again. I decided I should go and make amends, maybe even ask her if I could buy her a coffee or something, after all I did throw up on her roses and she didn't dob me into the boss. Man I was right, I'm still paying for that fucking incident, think I always will.

So anyway I spot her in the café but she was with that pretty boy that arrived in the shop that day I passed out and I'm not going anywhere near that.

Decided just to walk away before I have any more silly ideas and just got to the car when I heard a scream.

Some prick had knocked her to the ground and attempted to cut the strap on her purse, I ran over threating to punch the asshole in the head and he saw me running towards him and bolted. Unfortunately with her purse, anyway, that's not important, purses can be replaced, so I bend down to see if she was okay. Her busted ankle was bleeding through the thick sock she had on. The sock had a hole in it where she scraped it so if it's enough the blood is seeping through then the cut must be deep. The stupid excuse for a boyfriend has run off down the street after the purse thief and I shake my head.

He can't be that into her if he is stroking his heroism ego more, he didn't even stop to ask if she was okay.

Prick.

Now this is when I get to the whole fucking point of the story.

I'm trying to get her sock off and she is fighting me tooth and nail. I am trying to explain I need to see how bad it is but she is carrying on like I'm the one attacking her; her friend came out and also told her the same thing about getting the sock off but she is getting more and more anxious, in fact she looked like she was going to throw up again.

I asked her friend if she could go inside and call the police as this incident needs to be reported if she is going to need some type of compensation 'cos I'd say she won't be back at work for a while.

I try again with the sock but then all of a sudden it occurs to me why she doesn't want her sock off. Before she threw up all over my feet, she asked me why I had my feet exposed, it'd never even occurred to me until now. She cannot have her bare feet touch the ground or any element because it makes her physically sick. But here is the spooky thing, I dreamt this, I dreamt that a woman cannot touch the ground with her feet because it is traceable, but the male can because it's going to save her arse, although the males exposed feet still makes her ill. It's a reoccurring dream that often has me awake at night wondering what the hell it's about.

Seriously I thought I may have had a mental problem or something, I am convinced my dream is related to her so I said it to her out loud. I told her I know she has a phobia of her feet being exposed because it makes her vulnerable to being traced. I told her I had dreamt it.

And she knew; she knew what I was talking about.

Thank fucking god for that, otherwise she would have started screaming that a crackpot has a hold of her foot. She nodded and looked straight at me with understanding and shock that another person knew what was going on inside her head.

I don't know how long we locked gazes in mutual understanding but it felt like hours, I gently let go of her foot and suggested I take her to the hospital, where I hoped I could have a chat with her and finally get a grip on what I was talking about and get some understanding rather than booking myself into the funny farm.

The gaze was broken when her poncey boyfriend came back and handed over the purse. Fucking tosser; her face lit up when she saw him so I thought I'd better just let the moment go and leave, better that way anyhow. The realisation was just a bit too deep for my liking, back to my normal life of driving trucks and being a bitter old fart.

But as the week wore on it started to play on my mind how the fuck she would have known what the hell I was spouting on about.

I've been having these dreams ever since I could fucking remember; it involves a young boy and his mother. They have to go into hiding for some reason or another but there is a group of people who want the boy for whatever reason but they cannot track her down because the earth is fucked and choking in chemicals and that kind of shit, but they invented some high tech gadget that can detect her movement through the earth from the DNA that she left behind through the particular partials of her feet. The part I play in the dream is walking around in bare feet 'cos I don't carry the certain chemicals in my feet, therefore they cannot track me and I am able to get the mother and the boy to safety.

It's complicated when I say it out loud but in my dream it makes perfect logical sense. But I also know how to help her overcome her fear, there is a way around it and until last week I thought it was just a fucking science fiction dream. But if she is having the same dream then what the fuck is that about? Not that what happened in the dream will actually happen I mean that is the stuff movies are made off, but I haven't met anyone yet that is cautious of the imprint she leaves on this planet.

So as the week wore on I decided to go and check up and ask her for a coffee, I even looked up the shop's number in the phone book and jotted it down. But I had to go and deliver the café owners next door a glazed pot I was required to replace after I had run over it so on the way home I called into the shop, but her friend was there again, and said she had gone shopping. So I took that as a sign to let it go, probably wasn't anything in it anyway just a coincidence. I bet she hadn't even given it a second thought so why should I.

I am on my way home and thank god it's Friday 'cos I think I'll just sleep the weekend away, take it easy. Apparently I have another big week next week so it's a good idea that I do. My two ragdoll cats Eliah and Jay-Jay will be pleased to be let out of their enclosure, I have had them in it all day. Normally I leave the door into the house open and just lock the external enclosure door so I don't get any break-in's but the door to the enclosure needs fixing as it seems to either be loose or jamming, either way it won't lock so after my sleeping, that would be my job over the weekend.

Home sweet home. After parking the car, I collect the mail from the box and fantasize about sitting with a cold beer in front of the footy. I unlock the front door and throw my boots inside. I haven't worn boots for the trip home, gotta stop doing that as my socks are starting to wear out. Throwing the junk mail in the bin I make my way to my waiting babies in their outdoor enclosure expecting to be greeted by hungry cats but instead I freeze in horror at the scene confronting me.

**Kym**

And suddenly my life is going in a completely different direction.

A bit radical accepting his proposal considering I have only had a few dates with him, three in fact, counting this one, he did spend the entire week nursing me so not sure if that counts as a big date or a relationship but I am too old to waste time wondering if he is Mr Right. He is Mr Right now and everyone seems to like him. His collage friends tell me he is the nicest guy they have ever known so I guess his references check out. And he is obviously not worried that I'm slightly older than him.

I had a beautiful night but the alcohol was wearing off fast, leaving me with the biggest headache, so I told Nathanial I should go home and insist he stay at the ball. He wanted to get the taxi home with me to make sure I got home safe but I said I would be fine and this is his night so instead he phones Mandy to ask her to make sure she was there at the other end and then before I had a chance to even process what has happened, he told Mandy we were engaged.

This annoyed me, as Mandy is my friend and we hadn't even discussed telling anyone.

I don't know what Mandy's reaction was but I can imagine it would not be pleasant only for the fact it came from Nathanial and not me. Then he asked before I had to leave if he could announce it to his friends. I reluctantly agreed, I was more frightened that we would have to do a celebration waltz. I told Nathanial that was fine as long as I didn't have to dance; he playfully said he hoped I wouldn't ever have to dance again after showing off my dance moves.

After the big announcements to his friends they insisted we toast the occasion; then the girls bombarded me with questions of dates, dresses and themed weddings. It was getting too much so I excused myself and after Nathanial saw me off in the taxi promising me he will see me in the morning, I finally got some quiet thinking time to myself.

I didn't think that this was how I was going to get engaged and since I don't have a ring yet, it doesn't feel like I have confirmed anything. Well in fact I never thought I would get married to anyone. I was completely content and accepted I would be on my own without children and have Mandy's kids available to spoil whenever I felt like it. Now I see a whole lot of possibilities ahead, I could have a child and I could have a family home, I could have a white wedding, I could tick 'Mrs' on a form instead of 'Miss'. My whole life has just changed in an instant.

And it all started with a trip to the hairdressers. Giggling, I think I must find out which child put the card in the bathroom for me to find and thank them.

The taxi pulls up at home and Mandy is there at the front gate.

I take a deep breath and get ready to confirm the announcement that Nathanial rudely made to her; Mandy will have doubts about the engagement, not because she doesn't want to see me happy, she is just protective of me so I know she is going to tell me I am rushing into a commitment with someone that I have known for less than two weeks.

Nathanial pre-paid the driver so I don't have to worry about it, something I am going to have to get used to, someone looking after me. I step out of the taxi and instead of Mandy grilling me about Nathanial, she hands me a phone.

"You have to take this," she said, "he has been calling all night. He called the shop phone and it got diverted to my mobile, he is in some type of distress and said only you can help him. It involves birds."

Puzzled at Mandy's garbled explanation and the thrusting of the phone at me I thought it may have been Nathanial but got completely taken aback yet again when I pressed the phone to my ear and found it was the delivery driver; the one that gave me the ride home; the one I threw up all over; and the one that told me he knows why I have my phobia to exposed feet.

He said his name was Chris or something, he sound panicked and said he needs me to come to his place and help him, he said he is surrounded by birds and has been stuck to the same spot for ages.

I hung up to begin with, what a sick joke, that man clearly has problems if he thinks that is funny.

The phone rang again and Mandy suggested she block his calls, but I had to think again; it seems an unusual call and I should just make sure it's not a joke before I call the police and report him for harassment. After all I know he has a phobia of birds from the way he reacted towards Harry when he landed on his head; if he said a bird is loose in his house and he passes out, he could, I don't know, drown in his own vomit or something. Mandy agrees that does seem plausible so I answer him and he is more than distressed now, I think he *is* about to pass out. He said he is surrounded by birds inside his enclosure. I think that is a slight exaggeration, it's probably just one bird that had gotten through an open window or something and I presume when he says enclosure he means house.

I think he is overreacting to a bird that has flown into his house but I can feel his anxiety and I guess I should answer his distress call, don't think it's one for the emergency services so I guess I am it.

He tells me his address through his panic and I relay the address to Mandy who quickly jots it down on a piece of junk mail with the girls glitter pen left on the front porch.

After telling him I am on my way and hanging up from him Mandy insists it may be a good idea if she comes with me and gets Tamara over to watch the kids. But I really do not feel it's a job for two, even with Mandy's concerns for safety I think I will be fine, I joked with Mandy that if I was really concerned for my safety then I should take Harry with me for protection, she didn't see the funny side and thought it may be a good idea that I did. She gave me her mobile to take with me instead and gave me a quick lesson on how to use it.

Her anxiety is making me nervous, he doesn't seem to me as the type to attack me or lure me into a situation I am uncomfortable with but we have had a lot of run-ins with each other so maybe I have dented his ego and he does want payback. But even as I think it, it sounds absurd, but to comfort Mandy and her concerns I take the phone from her.

After a quick change from my ball gown to my old slacks with a crease down the middle and slipping on brown loafers with my stockinged feet I am instantly transformed back to my old self again. Funny how in one night my life has taken on the two different sides of me.

I feed Harry and my two canaries and think about the delivery man standing there frightened as a bird circles him, waiting for me to come and rescue him.

I'd better stop procrastinating and get there; I order another taxi and relay Mandy's glitter pen directions to the cab driver. I have no idea what I am doing but it feels crazy, I look down at my feet and feel a bit better back in these heavy shoes. Like I have stepped back into my cocoon after a short time out of it and it feels weird because I think I would be just as happy to step back into it.

We pull up outside a small but fairly tidy house. It turns out it's not far from my place, I pay the cab driver and make my way up the path. The atmosphere tonight seems weird, even on this beautiful evening; there is a sense of a calm before a storm.

I reach the door and can hear him yelling for help. I didn't waste time, I knocked first but I doubt very much he would be able to hear me. It does sound like an aviary in there and it sounds more like a flock of parrots rather than one bird that had flown inside. Feeling silly and not knowing whether or not to enter, I knocked on the front door again, this time harder. Feeling hopeless I gingerly try the handle, which was unlocked. Calling out to him announcing my arrival I step into a foyer.

I heard him call out again. I yelled back to him to tell me where he is. He seems relieved to hear from me and called me Kate, I placed Mandy's cell phone at the ready in my pocket and followed his voice.

A plover bird met me in the foyer room and swooped at me as it circled and flew around me, landing on a closed door from where the delivery man screams appear to be coming from. How in heaven's name did a plover bird get inside a house? But I guess that must be the bird causing him the distress and I cannot say I blame him, plovers do tend to feel threaten when trapped in confined spaces.

I open his front door to allow the bird to make its escape back outside. It flew toward the door but rested on the frame above. Not wanting to agitate it, I left the bird to find its own way out and went to tell the delivery driver the good news. Following his distress cries I open a door and was confronted by the most horrifying but hilarious scene I have ever witnessed.

The delivery man was standing in the middle of what appears to be a giant outside bird cage attached to the house and joined by an internal door. He appears frozen to the spot, looking so pale that flour has more of a tan than he does at the moment. Surrounding him were a least a dozen different species of birds, from magpies to wrens and even a pair of galas. It was so funny I couldn't help but giggle.

How could one keep birds and have a phobia to them.

He is pleased to see me and told me to shut the door quick. I pushed the internal door shut and giggled at his entrapment. But he is not amused by my giggling. I explained my amusement and asked why would he have a bird aviary and be frightened of birds; but my giggle was short lived when he sharply told me that it is not a cage for f'en birds, it is a day enclosure for his cats and he doesn't know how the f'en birds got in here.

Cats!

"You have cats?" I gulped, "are they in here?"

I look up and one is above my head on a makeshift plank. I look further and realise there are two of them; one is swiping at the birds as they teasingly swoop over the feline, the other is the one above my head.

I cannot move, now I am frozen to the spot, it's not that I am afraid they will come after me and attack me, nor am I allergic to them. It's the way they smooch around your ankles and feet, and the purring feels like a thousand razors cutting at my inner tolerance level. If they stay away from my feet, I'm okay.

"You have cats," I state in a calm voice to hide my hysteria, "well that's just peachy."

"Of course I have cats," he said, snapping at me, "they are meant to repel the fucking birds."

"Well it ain't working out," I said, my eyes fixed on them.

"So, you going to get me out of here?" he asked, "if I move, the birds will make a beeline for the door and I don't want them getting in my house."

"It's okay," I comforted him, "I have left the front door open, they will find their own way out."

"You left my front door open?" he said in disbelief.

"Yes, well I had to; you had a plover bird flying around your foyer."

"Well that's just great!" he said, "'cos the minute you open that door, my cats are going to get loose outside, hence this enclosure you have just trapped us in."

"What about that door?" I asked, spying the outside door from this enclosure leading to a backyard.

"That one is fucking jammed," he snapped.


I cannot believe his attitude; I am only trying to help. I told him his tone is one of complete rudeness considering I went out of my way, unsure whether or not he would attack me when I got here, only to be confronted by his cats that he never warned me about.

"Why should I warn you about my cats?" he snapped, "you didn't warn me about your stinking bird the day it landed on my head, now look what's happened."

"You're blaming me for birds getting into your enclosure?" I scoffed, outraged by his accusation. "That is completely absurd. How is that possible, I don't even know you."

He panicked again, crying out in terror as a bird swooped down on him as it flew across the enclosure.

"Okay, try not to panic," I advised, keeping an eye on his cats that are fixated on a small wren darting about the cage. "The more you panic, the more agitated they are, just try and keep calm, can you walk to me?"

"Oh my fucking god I think I am going to be sick," he said.

"Well so far you haven't," I said, "so you must be doing well. Now walk to me."

"I haven't been sick 'cos one hasn't fucking landed on me yet."

"Don't worry, they're wild birds, they're not going to go near you, except for maybe that butcherbird, they tend to be a bit friendlier."

He seems more agitated since I said that, I must really try and keep him calm. He is starting to shake at the galas landing by his feet.

"Just shoo the fucking things away," he said, getting panicked again.

His cats are getting bored now and are starting to walk towards me.

Oh god now I'm starting to panic.

"Call your cats please," I said.

"They won't hurt you," he said, breaking out in a cold sweat as the gala continues to circle him.

"Oh fuck," he said as realises my expression, "you're afraid of cats as well?"

"Well you're afraid of birds," I retorted in embarrassment, "and why did you call me anyway, why didn't you just call the emergency services?"

"Because you're the fucking bird whisperer," he said, "you are supposed to get me out of this."

"Since when?" I argued, "how are you my responsibility?"

He swore hysterically again when another bird flew past his ear and landed above my head, this stirred the cats up again and one of them started using my leg as a leaning post to get to the bird.

Its paws against my leg are making my skin crawl. This is not good, my breathing is getting laboured and anger is creeping up inside me.

Sensing my sudden silence as a sign of trouble the delivery driver tries to call the cats but they are fixated on the gala.

"Don't you pass out Kate," he panicked, seeing the distress on my face. I find my breath again.

"It's Kym," I wheezed, "my name is Kym."

And for the first time since my arrival he looks at me as if I am a real person and not some delivery customer.

"Cameron," he said, "great to fucking meet you."

Then his lips start to curl in amusement. This causes me to break into laughter at how absurd this situation was.

Two pathetic people trapped in a cage by harmless animals, afraid to move in fear because we are paralysed by some silly phobia in our heads.

Maybe that's it; it's all in our heads.

"Cameron," I said, still trying to cope with the fact the cat is kneading at my legs, "focus on me," I said. "Just look at me and focus on walking towards me."

"I can't," he said, "my legs feel like fucking jelly. And when I get to you, then what? The latch on the cage has jammed and my front door is open, what if my cats escape?"

"Well that is the risk you have to take," I said, "otherwise we are stuck here."

He thinks for a moment flinching with fear every time a bird makes a move.

"All right," he agrees, "we will open the enclosure door to outside, the yard is high fenced, with a bit of luck the cats will stay in the yard and that way the birds can fuck off."

Closing my eyes and willing my stomach to keep calm, I slowly step forward. I feel the cat's paws slip from my legs and I open my eyes to see they are no longer at my feet. I'm fiddling with the latch on the cage; it does seem to be jammed. The cats run towards the door, stirring up the birds again.

"Oh my!" I cry, trying to go back to my happy place as the cats dance around my feet waiting for me to open the door, and failing.

"What's going on, what are they doing?" I ask as I frantically fiddle with the cage, trying to push it off its latch.

"They think you are going to feed them," he said, "try not to let them out."

"Well how do you open this stupid door?" I screamed. This is hopeless, I start to feel weak but I have to get out of here now.

"You need to hit the latch with something heavy," he said.

"What do you propose is heavy?" I said with a hint of sarcasm to my voice.

"Your shoe?" he said.

Oh no way, that is out of the question.

"Look," he said in a soothing voice. "I know that your feet cannot touch the ground, but if you take your shoe off your foot doesn't need to."

"How do you propose that?"

"Because I am going to shuffle over," he said with a hint of bravery to his voice, "and when I get there you take off your shoe and lean on me, that way your foot won't touch the ground."

"But if you come over," I said through my laboured breathing, "the birds will follow once we open the door, they will all flock."

"Well I can't stand her for fucking ever," he said, "my legs are starting to go numb."

He slowly starts moving, dry reaching as he steps over the loose feathers on the ground in his socks. The cats become more excited as he approaches the gate, one brushes up against my feet and that was enough.

My legs lose it and me collapse to the floor. The horror as the cats smooch around my head made me cringe, until I realised as long as they are nowhere near my feet, I can cope.

Cameron grimaces as he reaches me, the birds still circling.

"Right, now I'm going to reach down and take your shoe off," he said, shooing the cats away, "just grip onto my arm and close your eyes."

He removes my shoes and it feels like someone has scraped their fingernails down a blackboard, the feeling inside me is pushing through me and now I can feel the cold breeze on my stockinged, exposed feet.

This is too close, my foot is resting on the concrete floor and it stinks of cats in here. I grip tighter to his hand and I feel him gently remove my hand and place it on his arm.

The birds have become completely agitated and distressed and they are starting to swoop more.

Cameron's panic is at an all-time high and he is barely functioning. I am trying to hold my exposed foot off the concrete but my leg is becoming increasingly tired. My eyes are still closed and I can hear the latch clanging as he hits it with my heavy shoe. The birds are loud and it is absolutely chaotic in here.

Then the birds go quiet, deadly quiet. Not daring to open my eyes, I ask Cameron if they had been freed.

"Not yet," he said, his voice full of determination as I hear another clang of the latch being struck, "almost there."

Then why have the birds' gone quiet?

Just then the earth below us jolts. It was so fierce it feels like the whole house was pushed sideways.

"What was that?" I ask nervously. Then the earth starts to shake.

"Fuck it's an earthquake!" Cameron said.

I opened an eye to see the wall starting to crumble around us. "Quick, head for the internal door," he added.

The shaking was so violent I could barely get my balance as I struggled to get to my feet and shift my weight. More debris fell down around the internal door. The cats seemed to be dodging the debris as they fall around them.

"We gotta get out of here!" Cameron said, "we'll have to go out this door," he shouted, giving the latch a final violent whack.

It fell open as the cats ran over my feet and out the door, followed by the birds.

Cameron covered his head as the birds flew out over the top of him.

"Come on," he yelled as the last of the birds flew overhead. My foot is dangling in the air and in order for me to move off the concrete I have to place in on the ground.

The earth is still shaking and I am willing it to stop. Apart from the fact my foot is exposed, I have never been so frightened in my life; I feel part of the house sink with an almighty bang, but even with an earthquake around me, I don't know if I can do it. I don't know if I can move.

"Give me back my shoe," I cry to Cameron.

"We don't have time," he said, "we need to get out in the open, and fast, I'm not trusting the fucking builder who built this fucking house right now."

He tries to help me but I won't move.

"All right," he yells, "then you'll have to crawl."

Taking his advice I kneel down and crawl out of the enclosure to the courtyard outside. Bricks from the porch are starting to fall and I freeze in fear.

"You have to run," he shouts, "Kym, look at me!"

I am so frightened I cannot comprehend what is going on, this earthquake feels like it is going on forever, don't they only last a few seconds?

"Kym!" Cameron yells.

I manage to glance at him and he's looking at me intently.

He grips my shoulders and looks deep into my eyes, "do you trust me; it was just a dream. All this fear and phobia is an illusion, it doesn't belong here."

And without a doubt there is no one else in this world that I trust more than Cameron. I nod at him intently and I feel him lifting me just as another brick falls near where my head was. He runs out to the middle of the backyard and places me down on my feet. We watch as more brinks fall, littering the enclosure.

Then the shaking stops.

We stand there for a few moments in silence. The cats come out from their hiding places, diverting our attention from the mess in front of us and I suddenly realise we have been holding on to each other for the last few minutes.

Cameron steps forward and picks up one of the cats to offer comfort, their wide eyes speak of the trauma they just experienced. I don't feel so much animosity for the cats any more as I watch Cameron cluck over them in relief, and it is such a beautiful sight to see, such a caring and loving person having affection for such another creature.

I start to giggle as my eyes adjust in the dark and dust.
"Um Cameron," I said, trying to hold my amusement, "you have a butcherbird hanging on to the back of your shirt."
I waited for the panicked reaction, but he merely points to my feet.
"Yeah, well look," he said.

I glanced down at my feet in the darkness, I wriggle my toes in the softness of the earth, I have lost my other loafer and my stockings are in shreds hanging off my feet. I stared in disbelief at the sight of my exposed feet, I don't feel afraid anymore and my future seems promising and bright; I can see possibilities for me beyond my expectations, I am destined for bigger and better things.

"Well I'll be," I said, marvelling in wonderment at my feet in front of me.
"So this is what the big drama has been about all this time," Cameron said as he starts to chuckle.

I can feel my lips starting to curl into a smile, through the adrenalin of the earthquake we realise what idiots what we have been. The dream we both dreamt was not about dark forces tracking me down through the imprint of my bare feet in the earth. The dark forces were simply a shadow of our own fear following us. The cycle of fear that expels humanity from the human race. Love, faith, and trust are what we were born with. Fear is what we learned here.

Cameron's chuckle has escalated into raucous laughter as his feathered friend climbs up onto his shoulder. I join him in mutual amusement, we are laughing so hard we are both hit the soft earth rolling around on the dirt. Two strangers that have complete trust and faith in each other without fear and without agenda.

**11**

*Earth Time: Year 2036.*

**Elizabeth**

Phoenix is now 20 years old.

And what a strapping, handsome man he has turned out to be.

His birth wasn't an easy one. With all that knowledge we had to install in his brain to grow and develop, his head was unusually big. But Kym coped well with having a child with a record head circumference; she and Cameron are proud parents who doted on him, but it wasn't easy raising him.

By the age of two he had mastered the art of phonics and by the age of eight he had graduated primary school. But as advanced as he was academically, it was his wisdom and insight that rallied all the peacemakers together and at the age of 16 he had a following bigger than the Jesus era and by the age of 18 had teamed up with a man in Texas and built a stargate to the new world.

Something that had been on the agenda of the High Council for 300 years but needed a Maharishi to deliver this beautiful portal to the adjoining worlds.

As I said, it wasn't easy raising Phoenix, but we were all on hand to help. Rebecca, Lizard, Gypsy, myself and yes even Larry. It was such a huge shift back in 2015 when Cameron and Kym got together, I remember the mission well.

We couldn't work out why such an important mission such as ensuring the conception and birth of a new peacemaker to lead us into a new world was given to us; a bunch of spiritual amateur's, all with egos and agendas of our own. And what was worse, was when they sent in a troll such as Larry to jeopardize it and make our job harder was something I couldn't comprehend.

I remember the evening well.
I discovered Bossman had sent in Larry to hinder the mission by steering Kym away from Cameron and into the arms of a nobleman called Nathanial. I couldn't help but wonder what the purpose of this was, until the answer was right there, it was simple; the reason the High Council put us into an important mission was to learn the values that humanity seems to have lost.

It was the same in the spirit world; we passed over into the spirit world without bringing with us the very thing we were born with.

The High Council has love, faith, and trust in us to deliver the most important thing to happen for the world to continue. The spirit world copped a lot of losses; a lot of spirits now don't exist in the universe at all. But it was necessary, some had lost their way. Especially those who had followed a religion that held no relevance to human life and when they passed over and found the religion did not deliver what was promised to them on earth. This only fueled distrust and anger in those spirits who influenced the physical people they were meant to be guiding.

It didn't take long to convince Rebecca we need to work together as one to ensure Cameron and Kym pass the hurdle that was needed to ensure their fate was sealed. This was a big step for Rebecca, especially when her existence was under review, perfection and orderly was all she knew. She had been programmed on earth to function in an orderly way that demanded nothing but perfection from herself, and that was something she carried over to the spirit world. Larry was also sent to teach Rebecca that life was not meant to function in an orderly manner.

Some things have to get thrown into chaos for the pieces to land in a way that is perfectly imperfect. It took a lot out of Rebecca to realise this, and accept it, especially accepting the lesson from an uncouth hobo such as Larry.

It really was hard to watch her growth and pain, but in the end Rebecca put aside her differences with Larry, accepted what will be will be, and agreed.

And as Larry says, just dance.

I still don't know to this day how Larry managed to stuff a couple dozen wild birds into Cameron's enclosure as birds are also people passed over into the spirit world that were reincarnated, and Larry hasn't exactly got a fan club in the spirit world, but I guess he won them over somehow and what a magnificent role everyone played that night of the almost fatal earth shake that could have wiped out all of humanity if Cameron and Kym didn't realise the most important thing on earth.

Love, trust and faith in each other.

It's magical here on top of this mountain, I look behind me at the earth we are about to leave behind for eternity. The war on religion had taken over the earth; those who hadn't gone back to their true heart are left behind in a world that has no value for humanity. Chemicals from the weapons and mass production of unsustainable products with intention to harm had polluted the earth have made many animal species extinct. There was no option left; earth had to go; it's time as a living planet was up; it would no longer sustain life.

The stargate to this new world is ready, and the bright and beautiful light it radiates is just peaceful. It really is a magical atmosphere; Kym and Camron are standing here, hand in hand looking at their son with pride. Many of the animal kingdom are here, and people, people as far as I can see, bound with a neutral love for each other. Even Nathanial, the boy Kym dated all those years ago, has found his true heart and is standing in much admiration for Kym.

The woman who he held on a pedestal with much gratitude for teaching him that to be a humanitarian is to have no personal agenda other than to serve others, that's why he was so drawn to Kym, it was a lesson he craved, and one she could give. And the night Cameron and Kym finally sealed their fate, Nathanial learnt the true meaning to be noble was to wish Kym happiness and let her go.

Where we are going, there is no money, there is no hate, there is no religion, life is pure and everyone is equal.

Decisions are made diplomatically, everything is available in abundance, and humanity has faith in each other.

Jesus is here, standing beside Phoenix, proud of the man who will carry on the vision from all those years ago, before fear, misunderstanding, and hate completely took over.

Jesus is looking forward to his new role in the new world, he is stepping down from the role of a healer to a more simple life, and will become the only milkman that will turn your water into wine if you place your glass bottles of water at the gate.

The stargate fires up and Phoenix invites everyone to step forward. The first to go through is Cameron and Kym, hand in hand with a love higher than the Highest Council has for humanity. A new day dawns as the people step forward through the stargate and into their new world.

****End*****